CELESTIAL CHAOS

BLACKMOORE SISTERS COZY MYSTERY SERIES BOOK 9

LEIGHANN DOBBS

CHAPTER 1

Something didn't feel quite right...

Morgan Blackmoore stood at the kitchen counter, a cup of coffee in her hand and a funny feeling buzzing through her entire body.

She paused, the mug halfway to her lips. A strange tingling raced across her skin, raising the hairs on the back of her neck. Her intuition—usually a gentle hum in the back of her mind—spiked sharply.

Something was off.

She glanced out the kitchen window above the sink. The herb garden stretched before her, neat rows of magical plants glowing softly in the dawn light. A light mist curled around the leaves and stems. Beyond the garden, the woods loomed dark and shadowy, the trees barely visible through the fog.

A flash of movement at the edge of the trees caught her eye. Belladonna, the family's sleek white cat, trotted purposefully into the shadows. Morgan frowned. Belladonna hardly ever went into the forest.

Unease unfurled in Morgan's belly as she sensed a sudden undeniable shift in her magical intuition. She took a deep breath and reached out with her senses.

She focused on letting her awareness drift outward. The currents of magic that usually flowed steadily around her were churning and chaotic. She probed deeper, trying to understand the disturbance. That was when she saw it—a faint glimmer pulsing through the magical currents. She narrowed her focus, willing the glimmer to take shape. It was something important—she could feel it. The glimmer solidified into a glowing orb, flickering and shifting, almost forming into...

"Penny for your thoughts."

Morgan jerked, the coffee mug slipping from her fingers and shattering on the floor.

She whirled around, heart pounding. "Luke! You scared me half to death."

Luke grinned, leaning against the kitchen doorway. "Sorry, didn't mean to startle you. You looked pretty deep in thought, though." His green eyes glinted with amusement as he took in the puddle of coffee and broken mug at her feet.

Morgan exhaled forcefully, pressing a hand to her chest. "It's okay. I was just..." She trailed off, frowning. The magical currents she'd been sensing were gone now, dispersed by Luke's sudden appearance. But those magical currents had been real, and she was certain they were an indication that things were not right.

"Just what?" Luke prompted.

"I don't know exactly," Morgan said slowly. "I was trying to get a sense of something... a disturbance in the magical currents. But then you surprised me, and I lost my concentration."

Luke straightened, his amusement fading. "A magical disturbance? Here in town?"

Morgan nodded. "It felt chaotic, like the magical energy was swirling violently. And my intuition was going haywire right before you walked in. Something's wrong."

She knelt and began picking up the larger shards of the broken mug. Luke grabbed a towel and mopped up the spilled coffee.

Morgan frowned as she dumped the broken pieces in the trash. "I'm not sure what it was exactly. My intuition doesn't usually spike like that over nothing."

Luke leaned back against the counter, arms crossed over his chest. "Well, it's probably not nothing. Dorian mentioned that some sort of celestial alignment is coming up in a few days. She said to be on high alert."

Dorian Hall was Luke's boss at the secret government paranormal agency for which he worked. The Blackmoores often did work for that agency.

"Celestial alignment?" Morgan echoed with a puzzled look. "What's that?"

Luke ran a hand through his shaggy dark hair. "I'd never heard of it either. She said it only happens once every five hundred years. Something about crystals on all the planets aligning. It creates a massive surge in magical energy across all the realms."

Morgan's eyes widened. "A magical surge? That would definitely explain the disturbance I was sensing." She chewed her bottom lip thoughtfully. "But why does Dorian want us on high alert?"

"The last time there was a celestial alignment, it left cracks between the magical realms that evil forces exploited to cross over to Earth," Luke explained grimly.

"Well, that sounds ominous."

Morgan turned to see her younger sister, Celeste, padding into the kitchen, stifling a yawn. Her blond hair was pulled up in a messy bun, and she was wrapped in an oversized knit sweater against the morning chill. She made a beeline for the fridge and started to pull out ingredients for her morning staple drink, a green smoothie.

"Have you heard of this celestial alignment?" Morgan asked her.

Celeste paused, carafe in hand. "Celestial what now?"

Morgan quickly recapped what Luke had said about the rare planetary alignment and its effects on magical energy. Celeste's ice-blue eyes widened as she listened.

"Huh," she mused, pausing to turn on the blender and then pour the pureed contents in a glass. "That's really weird. I wonder why we've never heard about this before."

Morgan shook her head. "No idea. But listen, did you feel anything strange this morning?"

Celeste tilted her head thoughtfully. "Now that you mention it, I did get a weird vibe when I woke up. Kind of an anxious, jittery feeling. Like the feeling I get when a ghost wants to talk, but no one was there."

"I sensed a disturbance in the magical currents," Morgan said. "My intuition went haywire right before Luke walked in. Something big is happening."

Celeste sipped her coffee, frowning. "Well, that's not good. Your intuition is never wrong."

Johanna Blackmoore bustled into the kitchen, her gaze zeroing in on the trash can. "Is that one of my favorite mugs in there?"

"Sorry, Mom." Morgan gave her a hug. "I dropped it."

Johanna waved her hand dismissively. "No worries. I have more." Then she turned her knowing gaze on her daughters. "What's going on? I sense you were discussing something serious."

Morgan quickly explained about the coming celestial alignment and the disturbance she had sensed in the magical currents. Celeste chimed in about the strange vibe she had felt upon waking.

Johanna's brow furrowed as she listened. When they finished, she nodded slowly. "You know, I think I might remember hearing something about a celestial alignment when I was a girl. It was very rare. I don't recall the details. If both of you felt something strange, that's significant. We need to pay attention to this."

Morgan felt a swell of validation upon hearing her mother confirm the importance of what she had sensed.

"We should check with Fiona and Jolene, see if

they noticed anything odd this morning," Celeste suggested.

"I'm heading to the shop soon. I'll ask Fiona," Morgan said.

"I'll see if I can get more information from Dorian," Luke added.

"Hopefully, she'll know more about this and what we should do." Johanna filled a mug, identical to the one Morgan had broken, with coffee.

"Yeah, hopefully, someone will." Celeste sipped her smoothie.

Morgan glanced out the window uneasily, looking at the spot where Belladonna had disappeared into the woods. "I think someone might, but unfortunately, it's not someone who can actually tell us what we should do."

CHAPTER 2

Fiona stared down at the strange iridescent yellowish stones that sat on the black-velvet tray on her workbench at Sticks and Stones, the store she shared with her sister Morgan.

She'd seen her share of semiprecious stones and crystals, both magical and not, but these were an unusual color and were behaving quite oddly. She watched as the stone zinged off the tray and hit the window. She'd never had stones that did that before.

The bells over the door chimed as a tiny woman wearing a hooded dark-green cloak entered the shop. It was early spring and still cool enough to wear jackets, but something about the woman seemed off to Fiona, though she couldn't quite place what.

Fiona quickly swept the bouncing stones into a

drawer and slid it shut. "Good morning! Can I help you find anything?" she asked brightly.

The woman's sharp gaze roamed over the cozy shop interior, taking in the rows of crystals and display cases full of jewelry that Fiona had made as well as the jars of dried herbs Morgan used for her concoctions.

"Quite an interesting establishment you have here," the woman rasped in a low, gravelly voice. She lowered her hood, revealing a deeply lined face and piercing silver eyes. "I'm looking for some jewelry for my sister, something very special."

Fiona felt unease prickle the back of her neck but kept her tone pleasant. "We do have some unique items. Is there anything in particular you're looking for?"

The woman drifted closer to the counter, the hem of her cloak brushing the worn floorboards. "Yes, you could say I'm searching for something quite... remarkable." Her gaze locked onto Fiona's as if peering into her soul.

Fiona suppressed a shiver, silently willing her sister to arrive soon. Dealing with this ominous stranger alone made her deeply uncomfortable.

Fiona nodded and walked around to the front of the display cases. "Well, we have quite a variety of gemstones and crystals, many of which have special properties," she explained.

Ping!

The woman's gaze jerked toward Fiona's desk. "What was that?"

"What?" Fiona played dumb even though she'd heard the noise too. "This cottage is old and creaky. Makes lots of noises." She pulled the woman toward the case farthest from her desk and pointed at a pink necklace. "This is rose quartz, known as the love stone. It's said to open up your heart chakra and promote unconditional love."

The woman peered at it, her expression unreadable.

Fiona set the pendant down and selected a ring set with labradorite. "This labradorite ring helps provide clarity and insight."

The woman's eyes narrowed slightly as she studied the ring. Fiona placed it next to the pendant and moved down the case. She picked up a bracelet made with variscite stones. "Variscite aids calm communication and brings harmony to relationships."

The woman let out an impatient huff. "Yes, yes, but do you have anything more... potent?"

Fiona glanced uneasily at her desk as another muffled *ping* sounded from the drawer. She coughed to cover the sound and quickly turned back to the woman.

"Potent in what sense exactly?" she asked, hoping to steer the conversation away from whatever was making noise in her desk.

The woman waved a bony hand impatiently. "Oh, you know, potent in bringing things together. Making connections. Influencing outcomes." Her sharp gaze bored into Fiona's.

Fiona's smile faltered slightly. She had a very bad feeling about this woman and whatever she was really after.

"I'm not sure we have anything quite that, um, potent," Fiona hedged. "Our gemstones have more subtle energies."

The woman clicked her tongue, clearly dissatisfied. "What a pity. Are you certain you have nothing more... impactful?"

Ping! Another stone ricocheted in the drawer.

Fiona crossed her arms, looking the woman straight in the eye. "I'm quite certain. Now, if there's nothing else I can help you find today..."

The woman stared at Fiona, her eyes narrowing. Then she glanced over at the desk, where the noises had come from.

"No, I suppose there isn't," she said slowly. She

turned and drifted back toward the door, pausing to look back over her shoulder at the desk. Fiona stood very still, resisting the urge to rush over and check on the stones.

With a swish of her cloak, the woman pushed her hood back up and opened the door. "Good day," she said crisply before disappearing outside.

Fiona let out a shaky breath as the door swung shut. She quickly returned to her desk and yanked open the drawer. The stones were pinging wildly off each other and the sides of the drawer. She scooped them up in her hand, holding them still, and felt a distinct vibrating energy pulsing through them.

What in the world *were* these things?

Fiona had barely had time to contemplate the stones when the bells over the door chimed again. She quickly closed her fist around the vibrating stones and hid them behind her back, bracing herself for another encounter with the ominous stranger.

But instead of the cloaked woman, her sister Morgan breezed through the door. Morgan paused and gave Fiona a strange look.

"What are you doing?" she asked, eyeing Fiona's awkward pose.

Fiona exhaled in relief. "Oh, it's just you," she said.

"Did you see a strange woman in a green cloak on your way in? She was just here acting very odd."

Morgan shook her head, her brow furrowing. "No, I didn't see anyone out there." She set the herbs she'd been carrying on the counter and turned back to Fiona. "Why? What happened?"

Fiona slowly brought her hand out from behind her back, opening her fist to reveal the stones, which were still faintly vibrating and pinging against her palm. She held them out to Morgan. "I was working on these stones to put in a bracelet, and they started going crazy and jumping all around."

Morgan's eyes widened as she took in the stones, which were now hopping up and down in Fiona's hand. "Are you making them do that?"

It was a fair question since Fiona had a way with all kinds of stones and could transmit energy to them to make them do as she wanted. She'd helped her friends in many paranormal battles with that ability. Except this time, she wasn't doing anything to make the stones move.

She shook her head. "They're doing it on their own and seem to want to go toward the window."

No sooner had she finished talking when one flew out of her hand and hit the window.

"Well, I guess that pretty much answers my question," Morgan said.

"Question?" Fiona picked the stone up from the floor and put them all in the tray then closed the lid.

"I was going to ask if you had noticed anything odd."

Fiona looked at the tray. "Um, yeah. But why?"

"I sensed a disturbance this morning." Morgan explained how both she and Celeste had felt something odd and then told her about the celestial alignment that Luke had mentioned. "I think whatever this alignment is, it's already affecting the magical energies. Making them act strangely."

"Makes sense. Maybe we aren't the only ones that know about it." Fiona glanced at the door and thought back to the creepy woman who had been so interested in potent magical objects.

Morgan gave her a knowing look. "You think the woman who was just here might be connected somehow?"

"I don't know," Fiona said uncertainly. "She seemed very interested in crystals and jewelry with strong magical energies. Kept asking if I had anything really potent or impactful. It was clear she was looking for something specific. Are you sure you didn't see her? I mean, you came in just a few seconds after she left."

Morgan glanced back at the door. "I didn't see a soul."

"Weird."

Morgan studied the tray holding the vibrating stones, her brow furrowed. "Where did you get these odd stones?"

Fiona shook her head, still perplexed by their strange behavior. "I bought them from Cal last month. Someone had pawned a whole box of loose stones and never came back to claim them. So he gave me a deal on the lot."

She leaned against the desk, arms crossed. "When I first got them, the stones seemed perfectly normal. I've worked some of them into jewelry already and they seem like normal stones. But these yellow ones..." She gestured at the tray. "... started acting like this today. Bouncing around and zinging all over. And that weird woman showing up right afterward, asking for something unusual for her sister? It can't just be a coincidence."

Morgan nodded slowly, thinking. "No, I'm sure it's connected somehow. Did Cal say anything about the person who pawned the stones? Anything unusual about them?"

"No, he didn't really have any details," Fiona replied. "He assumed they were just an amateur rock hound or something who'd fallen on hard times. Needed cash quickly and left the stones as collateral for a loan."

"Hmm." Morgan stared at the pinging, bouncing objects. "Well, someone out there obviously knows something about these stones that we don't. We need to figure out where they came from and why they're acting so strangely."

"Did Luke say that he got an assignment from Dorian about this?" Fiona rummaged in her drawers for a secure box for the stones.

"No, but she had mentioned it, and if we're all feeling something, then chances are we need to take some action," Morgan said. "I think we should go talk to Cal and see if he remembers anything else. And maybe do some digging, find out who pawned them originally. That might tell us something."

Fiona nodded resolutely. "I agree. Let me put these in something more secure." Fiona rummaged through her desk drawers until she found a small cedar box. "This should help contain their energy," she said, placing the vibrating stones carefully inside.

Morgan hurried over to her side of the shop and grabbed a handful of dried leaves. "These should mute the magic and calm the stones down a bit." She placed them carefully in with the stones.

Fiona added a layer of soft cloth to cushion the stones before closing the lid securely and tucking the box into the back of her desk drawer.

"What about the other ones?" Morgan asked.

Fiona pulled out a tray in which a colorful display of semiprecious gemstones sat. "These seem normal, but I'll keep an eye on them. All right. Let's go talk to Cal and see what we can find out," she said, grabbing her purse and keys.

Just as they reached the door, it suddenly burst open, the bells clanging violently. Fiona's heart skipped a beat when she saw who stood on the other side.

Sheriff White stood in the doorway, hands on her hips, glaring at them. Her salt-and-pepper hair was pulled back in a tight bun, matching the severe look on her lined face. She was new in town, and Morgan still hadn't decided whether she was friend or foe, but given the look on her face, she would have had to say that right now, the sheriff was definitely foe.

"Can we help you, Sheriff?" Morgan asked in her most innocent voice.

"I've received a report that you two are in possession of stolen goods," White said sharply, her piercing blue eyes flashing.

"Stolen goods?" Morgan said in surprise. "We have no stolen goods here."

The sheriff stepped inside, the floorboards creaking under her heavy boots. "That's not what Calvin Reed told me. He informed me that he sold a stash of stolen gemstones to Fiona, here." She leveled an accusing look at Fiona.

Fiona crossed her arms over her chest. "Cal wouldn't sell stolen goods. He sold me a box of loose stones, but he never said anything about them being stolen."

Morgan nodded emphatically. "Fiona got those stones over a month ago. If they were stolen, why didn't you come around then?"

Sheriff White's eyes narrowed. "Because we just tracked down where they ended up yesterday. They were stolen from Maynard Dove along with other family valuables."

Morgan's mind raced. She'd never heard the name Maynard Dove before. Was he some sort of paranormal connected to this celestial alignment? And if so, was he someone she would have to be wary of?

"Sheriff White, I swear I had no idea those stones were stolen," Fiona said earnestly. "Cal never told me anything except that someone had pawned them and never came back to claim them. I paid him in good faith."

The sheriff fixed Fiona with a hard look then glanced around the shop. "And where are these stolen stones now?"

Morgan crossed her arms. "Now wait just a minute, Sheriff. You can't just come barging in here, accuse us of theft, and take our things. We run a legitimate business."

Sheriff White bristled, putting her hands on her belt near her holstered gun. "I can get a warrant, but if you run such a legitimate business, then I'm sure you won't mind handing them over."

Fiona sighed and threw up her hands. "Fine. If it will get you out of here faster, I'll get you the blasted stones." She went to her desk and pulled out a carved wooden box. Opening it, she revealed a pile of smooth, polished stones in an array of colors—reds, blues, greens, purples. She held it out to Sheriff White with an exasperated look.

The sheriff took the box, eyeing the contents. She set it on the counter and pulled out a small receipt book, scribbling out a note. "Here's your receipt for the confiscated goods," she said crisply, tearing it out and handing it to Fiona. "I'll be in touch if I have any other questions. Don't be going anywhere, you hear?"

Fiona snatched the receipt with a huff. "Wouldn't dream of it," she said sarcastically.

Sheriff White tucked the box under her arm and strode out of the shop without another word. They watched through the window as she loaded the box into her squad car and peeled out down the street.

"Ugh, good riddance," Fiona grumbled, crumpling the receipt and tossing it on the counter.

Morgan shook her head, brows furrowed. "Something strange is definitely going on here. I think we need to get the whole family together to figure this out."

Fiona nodded grimly. "I agree. How about over a lasagna dinner tonight? I'll send a family text."

"Sounds good. Too bad we had to give up those stones. I feel like they might be a key to something."

"Don't worry." Fiona smiled slyly and reached into her bottom drawer and pulled out the cedar box. "I gave her the other stones, the ones that don't jump around. She doesn't need to know that she didn't get all of them."

Morgan didn't feel any more disturbances that day, so when she arrived home just before supper with garlic bread, she was starting to question whether she'd made too much of this whole thing.

"Maybe this will all blow over," she said to Belladonna, who had been sitting on the stairs in the foyer.

The cat slitted her ice-blue eyes and tilted her head. Morgan imagined she heard the cat say, "Nope." Or had she actually heard that? Lately, it seemed that her intuition had been expanding into being able to communicate with her favorite feline.

Morgan stepped into the warm, aromatic kitchen, where her mother and sisters were busy preparing dinner. Johanna took the garlic bread from Morgan, spread it on a sheet pan, and popped it into the oven next to a bubbling pan of cheesy lasagna.

"Something smells amazing in here," Morgan said, inhaling the rich scents of garlic, tomato sauce, and melted cheese.

Fiona tossed a salad with cherry tomatoes, cucumbers, and shredded carrots at the counter. "It's Mom's famous lasagna."

"My mouth has been watering all day," Morgan said, swiping a stray piece of shredded mozzarella from the counter and popping it into her mouth.

Jolene arranged plates and silverware around the large table. Celeste finished setting out glasses and filled a pitcher with ice water from the refrigerator.

"It's almost ready. Where are the guys?" Johanna asked, hands on her hips. A few wisps of dark hair escaped her loose bun.

Mateo came in through the back door, his boots clomping on the worn wooden floorboards. He gave Jolene a quick peck on the cheek as she arranged napkins beside each plate at the table.

Morgan smiled, seeing how happy her sister looked with Mateo. He caught Morgan's eye and gave her a subtle nod—their little secret acknowledgment. Morgan would never betray Jolene's fierce independent spirit by letting on how much Mateo watched over her.

Suddenly, two strong arms wrapped around Morgan's waist from behind. She let out a little yelp of surprise before recognizing Luke's familiar embrace.

"Geez, Luke, you're sneaking around here like some government agent," Morgan teased, twisting in his arms to give him a proper hug and kiss.

Jake breezed into the kitchen from the front hall, carrying a plain white bakery box. "Something smells incredible in here!" He gave Fiona a quick kiss on the cheek as she tried peeking under the lid of the mystery box in his hands.

"Ah ah ah, that's for later," Jake teased, holding the box just out of her reach.

Fiona playfully swatted his arm. "Fine, be that way."

Right behind Jake, Cal sauntered in, holding three bottles of red wine. "Wow, Johanna, you've really outdone yourself," Cal said, looking over the food on the table. "This lasagna smells heavenly."

"Thanks," Johanna said, blushing slightly. She took the wine and began pouring glasses for everyone.

The family settled into their usual seats. Morgan sat between Luke and Celeste, with Jake, Fiona, and

Cal across from them. Johanna and Mateo rounded it out by sitting at the ends of the table.

As they passed around the salad and lasagna, easy conversation and laughter filled the kitchen. Morgan looked around the table, her heart swelling at having everyone she loved together under one roof. But even through the light conversation, there was an ominous feeling because everyone knew they would be having a serious discussion after dinner. She just hoped whatever was in that bakery box would sweeten things up.

AFTER DINNER WAS OVER and the dishes were clean, Morgan settled into her favorite armchair in the sitting room, gazing out the big picture window overlooking the churning Atlantic Ocean below. The warm and cozy room was their favorite place to gather. While the rest of the house was decorated in antiques, this room was more modern, with comfy furniture and soothing colors in creams and sky blues.

Johanna curled up on the sofa, tucking her feet underneath her as she accepted a steaming mug of coffee from Jolene. Jake broke out his bakery box, which contained creamy cannoli. Everyone chose a seat and grabbed a cannoli while they discussed the celestial alignment and the strange happenings.

"We need to figure this out," Morgan said, leaning forward. "Clearly, there have been some strange magical occurrences happening lately that we can't ignore. The ominous vibes we've been getting and Fiona's mysterious jumping stones."

"Sorry about sending Sheriff White over," Cal said, turning to Fiona. "I didn't have much choice. White's all bluster anyway, and besides, we didn't do anything wrong. I had no idea that guy that pawned them was a thief."

Fiona waved her hand dismissively. "No problem. She's annoying, but I know she can't arrest us or anything. Besides, I actually kept the magical stones and a few others."

"Smart. I have a feeling they might come in handy," Johanna said. "Can we see them?"

"They're at the shop." Fiona chewed her bottom lip. "I guess we should have them here where we can watch over them."

The others nodded.

"Meow!" Belladonna rubbed her cheek against Fiona's calf, and the woman picked the cat up and settled her in her lap.

"It's clear we need more information. We need to

find out more about this Maynard Dove character," Celeste said. "Why did he have those vibrating stones in the first place? Did he know they were magical?"

Jolene nodded in agreement. "Maybe he acquired them without realizing their significance. The alignment could be activating their power."

"Exactly," Morgan said.

"We'll sniff out everything we can on this guy." Jake looked at Jolene, who nodded. Jake's private detective business could dig up details on anyone.

Cal picked up his phone. "I'll send you guys the name of the person who pawned them."

Mateo stood up from the sofa. "I'll ask around with my paranormal contacts and see what I can learn about the alignment and if they know anything about this Dove character."

Luke nodded. "I'll reach out to Dorian. See if I can get more specifics on the alignment. Should we meet again tomorrow night to compare notes?"

"Good idea," Morgan said.

"Sounds good," Cal added.

"I'll bring dessert." Mateo held up his cannoli.

Johanna stood up from the sofa, gathering the empty mugs. "It's settled, then. We'll meet here again tomorrow evening. I'll order pizza this time, though. I'm taking the day off from cooking."

Morgan smiled at her mother gratefully. She knew Johanna loved having everyone together and didn't mind making big family meals, but two nights in a row for this crowd was a big ask. "Thanks, Mom. You're the best. Pizza sounds great."

"Oh, and if anyone runs into a mysterious woman in a green cloak, use caution," Fiona said. "She came into the store looking for special jewelry, and I can't help but think she knew something about the stones."

Jake frowned, his investigator's instincts kicking in. "She didn't give you a name or anything?"

"Nope. And then she practically disappeared when she went out the door." Fiona glanced at Morgan, who nodded.

"She could have just been a woman looking for jewelry," Celeste said. "It is still cold enough for jackets and capes."

"True, but that would be a strange coincidence," Morgan said. "Anyway, looks like tomorrow is going to be a busy day. Better sit back and relax tonight." Morgan held up her cannoli and took a bite.

Belladonna jumped into her lap, fluffed her tail in Morgan's face, then looked back over her shoulder approvingly. It was good to know the cat condoned their plan of action.

CHAPTER 4

The next morning, Morgan knelt in the herb garden outside the kitchen. The sun had risen and was now sparkling off the waves in the cobalt-blue ocean. She took a deep breath of sea air, feeling invigorated.

"Meow!" Belladonna pawed at the thriving herbs in the earth.

"You know something, don't you?" Morgan asked.

Belladonna blinked slowly in response.

"Yeah, too much to ask that I could actually communicate with you." Morgan chuckled.

She turned her attention to a section in which the herbs seemed to be growing at an alarming rate. The leaves and stems stretched upward, and the plants appeared to have nearly doubled in size overnight.

Morgan was still examining the rapidly growing herbs when the back door creaked open. She turned to see her sister Fiona stepping outside, a mug of steaming tea in each hand.

"Thought you could use a pick-me-up," Fiona said, passing one of the mugs to Morgan.

"Thanks." Morgan wrapped her hands around the warm ceramic, breathing in the earthy aroma.

Fiona eyed the flourishing herbs. "Wow, they're really thriving already. It's so early in the season."

Morgan nodded. "I know. And it's only this one section too. The rest look normal." She furrowed her brow. "It must be related to all the strange magical occurrences lately. This celestial alignment seems to be amplifying things in odd ways."

Fiona knelt beside Morgan and gently brushed her fingers over the lush greenery. "Well, I guess we shouldn't complain about extra magical herbs. Could come in handy if things get really weird around here."

Morgan took a sip of tea. "You've got that right. We might need all the help we can get to figure this out."

"You've got me to help." Luke's voice came from the side of the house.

Morgan turned to see Luke coming toward them.

"I just got off the phone with Dorian," Luke said

after giving Morgan a peck on the cheek. "Apparently, this alignment is worse than we thought."

Morgan and Fiona exchanged a worried glance.

"She's been picking up some static about it, and we aren't the only ones experiencing strange occurrences," Luke continued. "Dorian said there have been historical cases with similar celestial events that resulted in significant paranormal activity."

"What kind of activity?" Morgan asked.

"Poltergeists, apparitions, evil entities getting through portals." Luke ticked each one off on his fingers. "General mayhem caused by surges in magical energy."

Morgan pursed her lips, thinking. "Well, that would explain the vibrating stones and the super-charged plant growth."

Fiona nodded. "And who knows what else is going to start acting up around here?"

Morgan turned to Luke. "Did Dorian say if there's a way to stop these strange occurrences from getting worse?"

Luke nodded, his expression serious. "She said the key is understanding how the celestial alignment works to amplify magical energy. Certain crystals act as amplifiers for each other. That's why all this magic is going haywire."

"So if we can find a way to disrupt that..." Fiona picked some stones up from the ground, and they glowed red in her hand.

"Do you think you can do that?" Morgan asked.

"Not sure. I need more information."

"What kind of information?" Luke asked.

"I need to know vibrating frequencies and how many stones align, and then maybe I can figure out if there is a stone that would lower the frequencies or block the energy from the other stones," Fiona said.

"I can ask Dorian about that," Luke volunteered.

"Is she sending us out on assignment, then?" Morgan asked.

Luke stared at her for a few beats. "Sort of."

"What's that mean?"

"She's not sending you out. The assignment is right here in Noquitt."

"Here?" Fiona glanced around. "You mean the paranormal chaos and turmoil is going to be right in our own backyard."

Luke nodded slowly. "Afraid so, and it's up to you guys to make sure it doesn't get out of hand."

FIONA LEFT Morgan and Luke in the garden and wandered back into the old house, her mind racing with thoughts about how to stop the impending crystal attack.

"There's got to be something I can do," she muttered to herself as she paced the creaky wooden floors. Because she was the sister gifted with stone magic, the responsibility would likely fall to her. Her mind raced over the information Luke had relayed from Dorian.

She sighed and flopped down into a dusty armchair in the formal living room, staring up at the intricate floral carvings on the ceiling. "Think, Fiona, think," she urged herself, tapping her fingers on the armrest. What stones could help block the sinister crystals? How could she use her powers to protect her siblings? Could she lower the frequencies of the amplifying stones with stones that would absorb some of the energy?

Her thoughts were interrupted by strange noises from the library across the main hall. She crept to the door and peered in.

Celeste sat cross-legged on the jewel-toned Oriental rug, eyes closed, humming tunelessly. Fiona winced as Celeste's ice-blue eyes popped open.

"Gah!" Fiona yelped, stumbling back. "Sorry. Didn't mean to disturb your meditation."

"No worries. Come on in," Celeste said, waving lazily. "I was done anyway."

Fiona edged into the room. "Were you communicating with spirits?"

"Yeah, just chatting with Rebekah," Celeste said with a sly smile.

"Who's Rebekah?" Fiona asked, eyebrows raised.

Celeste shrugged nonchalantly. "Oh, just one of our ancestors. I figured someone from way back might know about this whole celestial alignment thing."

Belladonna sauntered into the room and rubbed up against Celeste's leg. Celeste smiled and gently stroked the cat's fur, eliciting a satisfied purr.

Fiona pressed her lips into a thin line. "I don't think this house was even around five hundred years ago."

"Yeah, I know," Celeste said. "It was a long shot anyway."

"Well, Luke said this alignment could get ugly," Fiona said, lowering her voice. "He said paranormal disturbances will be at an all-time high, with the epicenter right here in Noquitt."

Celeste's eyes widened. "Ground zero for supernatural chaos," she whispered dramatically.

"Did Rebekah tell you anything useful at all?" Fiona asked.

Celeste shook her head. "Nah. She just kept showing me this weird sextant thingy."

Fiona furrowed her brow. "Sextant? Like for old sailing ships?"

"Yeah. No idea what that was about," Celeste said with a shrug. "Ghosts can be weird. I'm getting together with Cal for lunch. I'll text you if he finds anything interesting about the guy who pawned the stones."

"Thanks. Speaking of stones, I guess I better get to work and check on them. Hopefully, they didn't break out of the box and ping around the shop all night."

CHAPTER 5

Fiona parked her Jeep in front of Sticks and Stones. The small cottage was spruced up for spring. She and Morgan had removed the dead leaves from winter and planted fresh pansies in the cheerful yellow window boxes. The pansies loved the cooler weather and were thriving.

Morgan's car was in the small gravel parking lot along with a dark-green Prius. Fiona peered through the large front window as she approached, wondering if it was the woman in the emerald-green cloak again. But no, it was just Mr. Crawford buying his usual weekly basket of herbal teas.

The door chimed cheerily as Fiona entered the shop, just as Mr. Crawford was leaving with a brown paper bag in hand.

"Hello, Fiona." Mr. Crawford nodded politely to her.

"Mr. C! Good to see you," Fiona replied warmly. "Tell your wife I almost have those amethyst earrings done for her."

"I will. Thank you." He nodded once more to Morgan, who stood behind the counter, and headed out to his sedan.

Fiona closed the heavy wooden door behind her.

"Meow!"

Fiona whirled around to see Belladonna perched primly on one of the wicker chairs near the window. "What in the world? I just saw her lazing in the sun at home not ten minutes ago!"

Morgan shrugged, unperturbed. "She seems to appear in the strangest places lately. I guess we need to accept that."

"I guess so." Fiona looked at the cat warily.

Belladonna licked a paw and wiped it behind her ear, the picture of innocence.

"Has anything happened with the...?" Fiona angled her head toward the desk.

"Not a peep," Morgan said, shuffling through the receipts scattered on the long antique table she used as a workspace.

"I'll take a peek," Fiona replied, striding over to her

cluttered desk in the corner. She slid into the creaky wooden chair.

Belladonna leapt gracefully onto the desk, fixing her unblinking ice-blue eyes on the carved wooden box. Her tail swished back and forth as she stared. Fiona lifted the lid. The stones inside jumped and jiggled, much to Belladonna's delight.

Belladonna meowed as a few stones leapt out of the box and went pinging around the room. She batted them around the desk, playing with the enchanted objects. They bounced and rolled across the floor as she happily chased them.

"Belladonna, stop that!" Fiona scolded, slamming the lid back down.

But the cat just meowed defiantly and continued her game, pouncing on the stones and swatting them under the desk.

"Those aren't cat toys!" Morgan crawled under the desk to collect the stones while Fiona shook her finger at the cat.

Belladonna flicked her tail and sat back on her haunches, fixing them both with an innocent stare.

The stones pinged at the window one by one then fell to the floor and lay there without further movement.

"What was that about?" Morgan asked, crouching to gather the ones scattered under the desk.

"I don't know, but they seem to like the window," Fiona said, staring down at the motionless stones. "They pinged off it before."

Morgan walked over and peered out the window. "Do you think they could be part of this celestial thing and are trying to tell us something?"

"Maybe," Fiona said. She scooped up the last few stones and dropped them into the box, slamming the lid shut before Belladonna could pounce again. "I'll keep these in the drawer until we go home and give them a safer hiding place."

The cat trotted over to a blue-velvet chair instead, leapt up gracefully, and curled into a ball. She fixed them both with an innocent stare as if she hadn't just been batting mystical stones around the room.

The bell over the door chimed, and Fiona looked up, her stomach plummeting when she saw Sheriff White.

"Afternoon, Sheriff," Fiona said brightly. "What brings you here? In need of an herbal remedy or maybe some jewelry? I assure you it's not stolen."

Sheriff White did not return the smile. She stood stiffly just inside the entrance, hands on her utility belt. "I'm not here for earrings or tea, as you well know," she said sharply. "I'm here about some stolen gemstones."

"Again?" Morgan gave an exaggerated frown. "You came here about that yesterday. Maybe you *do* need some herbs. Ginkgo biloba or ashwagandha. They help with memory. I have some on hand."

"We handed over all the stones to you yesterday." Fiona waved the receipt in the air.

Sheriff White's eyes narrowed. "You handed over *some* stones. But Maynard Dove claims some are still missing." She looked sharply from one sister to the other. "Would you happen to know anything about that?"

Fiona shook her head, widening her eyes innocently. "Oh no, we handed over everything we had."

"We would never keep stolen goods," Morgan added earnestly.

Sheriff White studied them both with suspicion. "Well, if any more of those stones turn up, you'd better let me know quick. I'll be keeping an eye on you two." She turned abruptly and left, the door slamming behind her.

Fiona let out a breath as the door shut. She exchanged a worried glance with Morgan. Fiona sighed and leaned back against the counter. "Sheriff

White really needs to lighten up. She has no sense of humor."

Morgan shook her head as she tidied up some incense bundles on a nearby shelf. "Maybe if we didn't antagonize her all the time, she'd be nicer to us."

"You're probably right," Fiona admitted. She paused, furrowing her brow. "But anyway, this is bad news. If Maynard Dove knew those stones were missing right away, he might also know they're magical."

Morgan turned to look at her sister, concern crossing her face. "You're right. And if he is magical, then he might know we have them."

Fiona nodded, chewing her lip. "All the more reason to get them home as soon as possible, where we can use some magic to hide their existence. I'll message Celeste and see if she can come up with some sort of protective spell for them."

Morgan agreed. "We'll have to be extra careful transporting them. Maybe I can come up with an herbal concoction and surround them with it to dampen their energy. That *seemed* to work yesterday."

"Good idea," said Fiona. She glanced around the shop warily. "I don't feel comfortable leaving them here, even in the locked drawer. As soon as we close up, let's get them secured at the house. In the meantime, I'm going to look through my other stones and see if there is anything that can help us tamp down this alignment."

Morgan nodded. They would have to be vigilant until the stones were safely hidden away. Who knew what Maynard Dove would do if he discovered the truth?

CHAPTER 6

Celeste muttered under her breath as she rifled through the dusty tomes in the family library. Her sister Fiona had sent an urgent text about protecting the strange vibrating stones they had discovered. According to the ancient texts Celeste consulted, a simple barrier spell should do the trick, but only if constructed properly.

She gathered a handful of ordinary rocks from the garden and arranged them in a circle on the large oak table. Beside the rocks, she placed a bowl of salt, a vial of dragonfly wings, and several sprigs of rosemary. After reviewing the spell one last time, Celeste took a deep breath and began the incantation, waving her hands over the assembled items. The rocks trembled slightly, but nothing more happened.

Celeste huffed in frustration. Perhaps her pronunciation was off? She tried again, overenunciating the mystical words. The rocks shuddered more violently before the spell petered out. She was getting closer.

On a hunch, Celeste returned to the kitchen and grabbed a few more ingredients—a dash of black pepper and a spoonful of olive oil. She combined these with the other items and attempted the spell again. This time, the rocks floated upward, glowing faintly, before settling back on the table, encased in a shimmery barrier.

"Yes!" Celeste cried out in relief. With the proper adjustments, the protection spell had worked. Her spell making was improving!

Celeste was just cleaning up the remnants of her spellcasting when her phone rang. She glanced at the screen and smiled when she saw it was Cal.

"Hey, you," she answered warmly.

"Hey, yourself," came Calvin's smooth voice. "I was thinking of getting some lunch at Fresh and thought you might like to join me."

Celeste's stomach rumbled at the mention of food. All that magical effort had left her famished. "Funny you should say that. I'm absolutely starving! Fresh sounds perfect. I've been craving one of their Buddha bowls all week. Meet you there in fifteen?"

"It's a date," said Calvin. "It's warm today, so I'll get us a table on the patio. See you soon."

Celeste quickly tidied up the library and grabbed her purse and a light jacket. She'd had success with her spell, and now she was meeting her favorite person for her favorite lunch. Despite the ominous cloud of the celestial alignment hanging over her, the day was looking up.

Celeste strolled down Main Street, taking in the charming storefronts. Awnings shaded the large windows of the antique buildings that housed the quaint village shops. Window boxes overflowed with early blooms of pink petunias and purple pansies, their sweet fragrance mixing with the faint salty air blowing in from the nearby ocean.

As she approached Fresh Bistro, Celeste spotted Cal sitting at one of the wrought iron patio tables under the green-and-white umbrella. The patio was bathed in sunlight, warm for early spring. The tangy scent of fresh lemon and herbs wafted from the restaurant's open windows. The quiet murmur of conversation was punctuated by the clinking of silverware. She stepped onto the smooth gray pavers, weaving between tables draped with crisp white linens.

Cal stood up with a smile as Celeste approached. Behind his glasses, his eyes crinkled at the corners.

"Thanks for suggesting lunch." Celeste leaned in for a quick hug, breathing in his familiar scent of soap and cinnamon.

They settled into the wrought iron chairs across from each other. A server appeared with menus, the pages crackling as they browsed. Celeste sipped ice water, the condensation cool against her fingertips.

Celeste's eyes skimmed the menu as she deliberated between the Buddha bowl and lemon chicken salad. She'd been craving the Buddha, but now that she was here, she was too hungry to decide. She peeked over the top of the menu at Cal. "How's your day been so far?"

Cal set down his menu. "Pretty good. No visits from Sheriff White, so that's a win." He chuckled. "How about you?"

"Well..." Celeste lowered her voice. "Actually, things have been a bit strange. Luke came by with a warning about the celestial alignment. Apparently, it could amplify magical energy more than we thought." She leaned across the table, fingers curling around the cool metal. "Dorian wants my sisters and me to figure out how to keep things from getting out of hand when it happens."

Cal's eyebrows rose. He reached over and laid his hand comfortingly over Celeste's. "That sounds serious. Don't worry. Whatever you need, I'm here to help." His thumb gently stroked the back of her hand.

Celeste felt a rush of gratitude for his unwavering support. He always helped on their assignments, no matter how dangerous they were, and she was grateful. "I knew I could count on you." She gave his hand a grateful squeeze.

The waitress appeared, notepad in hand. "Ready to order?"

Celeste sat back, retracting her hand. "I'll have the lemon chicken salad, please."

Cal smiled at the waitress. "And I'll take the club sandwich. Thank you."

As the waitress walked away, Cal pulled his phone out and leaned toward her. "Speaking of helping, I looked back through the surveillance at the shop and found the video of the guy who pawned the stones. His name is Alex Summers, and I gave his info to Jake already." He turned the phone to face her and let the video play.

Celeste leaned in, eyes fixed on the small phone screen resting on the bistro table. The antique shop's interior came into focus, its shelves crowded with vintage clocks, silver trays, and faded books. A man approached the front counter wearing a knit cap pulled low and a nondescript black winter coat. He was average height, unremarkable.

Celeste watched the transaction unfold. The man had a bag of stones, and he dumped them on a black-velvet tray that Cal had laid out on top of the counter. Cal spent some time examining them. None of the stones did anything unusual and didn't seem magical at all. Nothing seemed amiss as the man accepted a stack of bills in exchange.

Celeste squinted, about to sit back. Then she caught a flash of emerald green at the periphery. "Wait! Rewind that."

Cal tapped the screen, reversing the video a few seconds. They both spotted it—outside the shop window, a figure in a flowing emerald cloak passing briskly across the frame.

"Didn't Fiona say to beware a woman in a green cape?" Cal asked, brow furrowed.

Celeste sat back heavily in her chair, lips pursed in thought. "She did, but there must be more than one person in Noquitt with a green cape." She drummed her fingers on the table. "It seems an odd coincidence, but it could just be a random shopper."

Cal rubbed his chin, considering. "I suppose it's possible. But it seems like there are too many coincidences in this case. Makes me nervous."

"Yeah, me too."

Celeste savored the last bite of lemon chicken salad, the citrus mingling with the rich avocado and crunchy pecans on her tongue. She dabbed her lips with the linen napkin and set it on her empty plate.

"That hit the spot. I'm stuffed," Cal said, leaning back in his chair contentedly.

Celeste nodded in agreement. "It was delicious. We'll have to come back again soon." She glanced at her watch. "I should probably get going. Lots to do before tonight."

Cal signaled for the check and pulled out his wallet. "It's on me today," he said with a smile. Celeste started to protest, but Cal held up his hand. "Please, it's my treat."

"Well, thank you. That's very sweet of you," Celeste said. She stood, smoothing out her flowing bohemian skirt.

After Cal paid, they stepped onto the street and strolled leisurely down the sidewalk past the other restaurants and shops.

"I hope your mom gets double pepperoni pizza tonight," Cal said. "That's always the best."

Celeste chuckled. "You know my mom will get at least one veggie for Mateo."

"And one with mushrooms for Morgan."

Celeste nodded. They each had their preferences when it came to pizza. "What do you think Mateo will bring for dessert?"

"Knowing him, probably one of his famous banana bread loaves," Cal replied. "But hey, maybe we'll get lucky and he'll bake something chocolatey instead."

Celeste's eyes lit up. "Ooh, chocolate—now you're speaking my language!" She chuckled. "Mateo's banana bread is amazing, but I could really go for some double chocolate brownies right about now."

Reaching the corner, Celeste and Cal paused. "I guess I'll see you tonight, then," Celeste said.

"Looking forward to it." Cal pulled her in for a quick hug. His navy cotton shirt felt soft against Celeste's cheek.

Tap, tap!

Celeste pulled back from Cal's embrace and glanced up at the weathered redbrick facade of the building next to them to the second-story window, where faded gold lettering on the rippled glass read "Cooper Investigations."

Behind the window was Jolene, waving to them.

She smiled, waving back. Beside her, Cal also lifted

his hand in an acknowledging gesture. Even from the sidewalk two stories below, Celeste could see the corners of Jolene's eyes crinkle in a wide, cheerful grin. Her voluminous brown tresses bounced as she made herself known to them.

Celeste pictured Jake sitting at his desk just out of view, likely shaking his head in amusement at his partner's antics. She knew their shared private investigation office had an ideal vantage point to watch the comings and goings below on Main Street.

Jolene gave them a thumbs-up and mouthed "See you tonight!" before disappearing from the window.

Celeste turned back to Cal and gave his arm an affectionate squeeze. "Thanks again for lunch. See you in a few hours."

CHAPTER 7

Jolene turned away from the window. Jake was leaning back in his squeaky leather chair behind the heavy oak desk, feet propped up casually amid the organized mess of case files and paperwork. Their office was a throwback to the old hardboiled detective era, with dark wood panels and frosted glass doors stenciled with their names. Jolene loved the old-fashioned vibe.

"What's going on out there?" Jake asked, not looking up from the file he was skimming.

"Just Celeste and Cal." Jolene sat back down at her desk and craned her neck to look outside. Celeste and Cal were gone.

Jake glanced up. "Looks like I found something on Alex Summers."

Jolene leaned forward in her chair. "What?"

Leaning back, Jake laced his fingers behind his head. "The guy who pawned the stones. Turns out Summers used to work for Maynard Dove a while back. Guess they had some kind of falling out—found a record of a police call between them that didn't go anywhere officially."

Jolene's eyes widened. "A falling out? Over what?"

"Doesn't say exactly." Jake shrugged. "But it got heated enough that the neighbors called the cops. No charges filed, though."

Jolene pursed her lips, thinking. "You think it could be something paranormal related?"

Jake looked over at her. "I doubt the Noquitt police would recognize that kind of thing if it slapped them in the face."

Jolene nodded. "Right."

Jake looked back at his computer screen. "From the report, it looks like a standard noise complaint. Nothing too out of the ordinary."

Jolene leaned back in her chair, tapping a pen on her notepad thoughtfully. "I hope Mateo or Luke have been able to dig up more on this Dove character. It's not like we can just google 'paranormal details' to get the scoop on him."

Jake nodded in agreement. "Guy's a tough nut to

crack. Rich as hell, that's for sure." He flipped through a file on his desk. "And old, too, though we couldn't find an actual birth date, which is pretty weird."

"Yeah, definitely seems like a red flag for something paranormal there," Jolene said. She scribbled some notes. "He does seem to donate a lot to charities and nonprofits, though, according to what I could find."

"Lots of wealthy folks do that to keep up appearances," Jake said cynically. "Doesn't mean much."

Jolene chewed the end of her pen. "Still, you'd think a guy with his money wouldn't care so much about some semiprecious stones. I mean, they weren't worth a huge amount monetarily."

Jake raised an eyebrow. "Unless their value lies somewhere else..."

"Exactly. We know those stones are magical somehow and presumably related to this celestial event. If Maynard Dove is one of the bad guys trying to open portals or whatever this event does, he would want those stones badly."

Jake leaned back in his chair, frowning. "He could be dangerous. We need to be careful."

Jolene clutched the obsidian amulet she wore around her neck, feeling its smooth, cool surface.

Fiona had made one for each of the sisters, designed to bounce bad energy back at the sender.

"Don't worry. We can take care of ourselves," she said confidently.

"I know, but Luke called earlier and said this might be worse than we thought. Apparently, Dorian has been hearing a lot of static about it through her various contacts, and similar events have caused adverse paranormal activity."

"Well, that's definitely not the news we were hoping for," she said. "It sounds like Dorian is anticipating something serious."

Jake rubbed his chin, his normally cheerful expression replaced with a grim look. "Yeah. Luke said she was very adamant that previous alignments like this have resulted in significant supernatural mayhem. Portals opening, dark forces slipping through, general paranormal chaos. Bad stuff."

Jolene, ever optimistic and confident, simply shrugged. "We've dealt with bad stuff before."

Jake gave her a small smile. "That's the spirit. This crew has handled its fair share of paranormal problems before. I reckon we'll all find a way through this too."

Morgan passed the pizza boxes around the kitchen table, the smell of oregano and tomato sauce mingling with the scent of the early blooming lilacs Johanna had cut from the garden.

Belladonna sat in the corner near her food bowl, watching them intently.

"So, what did everyone learn today about this celestial alignment?" Morgan asked before taking a bite of mushroom pizza.

Mateo cleared his throat. "Well, from what I gathered, it has to do with the alignment of ancient ley lines and crystals. Apparently, the lines are invisible to most, but they conduct magical energy. At the ends of the ley lines are certain crystals, and when the ley lines converge during the celestial event, it amplifies the energy flowing through them. Historically, that allows a lot of unwanted paranormal happenings, just like Dorian said."

"So we need to be prepared for anything—strange visions, objects acting oddly, time distortions?" Morgan asked.

"Yep." Mateo reached for a slice of pizza.

Jolene piped up next. "Okay, but how does Maynard Dove fit into all this? I did some digging, and he's quite wealthy and a bit mysterious. Old hermit type. Could be a paranormal, but I'm not sure."

Fiona leaned back in her chair. "Oh, he's definitely paranormal. Sheriff White came by the shop again today. Apparently, Maynard complained that the magical stones weren't in the lot I gave White yesterday."

Johanna nodded slowly. "Clearly, this Maynard knows what those stones are meant for if he was looking for them specifically."

"But what are they meant for?" Morgan asked. "That's the real question here. We need to figure out their purpose."

Jolene set down her pizza crust. "You're absolutely right, Morgan. Those stones are key in all this somehow. We need to study them, see if we can unlock their secrets."

"No problem. They're here at the house, locked away in a box," Fiona said. "Morgan lined the box with vervain to help dampen the magic. And Celeste did a protection spell around it, so the stones should be secure for now."

Morgan picked up her glass of iced tea and took a long sip before continuing. "I say we focus on learning more about this Maynard character and the cloaked woman. Did anyone run into her today?"

"I sort of did," Celeste said.

Morgan turned to Celeste. "Sort of?"

"I saw her on the surveillance video that Cal showed me of Alex Summers pawning the stones."

Fiona leaned forward, her brow furrowed. "Can you describe anything about her at all? Height, build, anything?"

Shaking her head, Celeste replied, "No, sorry. It really was just a quick glimpse of a green cape as someone moved past the window outside. But with everything else going on, it seemed too odd for it to be a coincidence."

"Hmm, that is strange," Morgan mused. She took a sip of iced tea before continuing. "What about this Alex Summers character? He's the one who apparently stole the stones from Maynard. Do you think he's involved in this celestial alignment?"

Mateo finished off his slice and patted his lips. "Doubt it. He must not have known the stones were magical, or he wouldn't have pawned them."

Jake set his plate on the counter. "If he worked for Maynard, he might know something useful about all this."

"Well, of course, I had to give his name to Sheriff White, so he's probably in jail right now," Calvin said. "He's on the tape caught red-handed."

"I still have some contacts down at the sheriff's station," Jake offered. "I can try to arrange a chat with Alex, see what details I can get out of him about Dove and the stones."

"Good idea." Mateo turned from where he'd been busy at the counter with a tray of cookies. The sight of the decadent chocolate chip, peanut butter, and oatmeal raisin cookies lifted everyone's spirits.

"These cookies are heaven," Morgan said through a mouthful of chocolate chip. She popped the last bite in and reached for a second.

Jake let out a low whistle as he bit into an oatmeal raisin. "Did you make these?"

"Actually, I did." Mateo beamed, pleased at the reception of his baking.

Belladonna's nose twitched. She crept forward, licking up a fallen crumb. Morgan laughed and tossed her a tiny piece of cookie, being careful not to include any chocolate.

"That was great." Celeste brushed peanut butter cookie crumbs off her fingers. "But I think it's time we checked out these stones."

"I'll go grab the box from the library." Fiona pushed back her chair and stood up. Belladonna scampered after Fiona's heels as she left the room.

The rest of them sipped their drinks and ate another cookie. A few moments later, Fiona reappeared holding a wooden box.

"Well, here they are." Fiona set the box in the middle of the table.

Celeste leaned forward, rubbing her hands together briskly. "Guess I'll remove the protective spell so we can open it up."

Belladonna let out a loud meow as Celeste began murmuring an incantation under her breath. She slowly waved her hand over the box, and Morgan saw a brief shimmer in the air.

"There, that should do it," Celeste said.

They all stared at the box apprehensively. Finally, Jake reached out and carefully lifted the lid. Inside, nestled on a bed of herbal leaves, lay the stones. Six were small, smooth, and varying iridescent shades of yellow, and two were a smoky white. All were completely still and ordinary looking.

Belladonna chirped and stood on her hind legs, front paws on the table, as if to get a look.

Johanna rubbed between the cat's ears. "What do you see? You probably know exactly what these are for."

Belladonna chirped up at Johanna and purred.

"Hmm, no vibration or jumping around this time," Fiona mused as she gingerly picked up a stone.

"So what's next? We need to figure out where these stones align and then what to do with that information to stop the negative paranormal forces from breaking through," Jolene said.

"According to what I found, there is one center stone. All the lines go there. If we can figure out where that is, then maybe we can put a spell on that crystal or replace it with something that absorbs negative energy."

Mateo's suggestion was met with a strange sound from the box on the table.

Morgan's gaze riveted on the yellow stones, which were shimmying and bouncing around in the box.

"Whoa, look at them go now," Fiona said.

"It's like our attention somehow activated them,"

Jolene added, her brow furrowed as she studied the jittery stones.

"So what's our next move here? I feel like we're on the edge of a breakthrough with these things," Morgan said.

Celeste perked up. "I can try to contact a ghost that might have been around the last time this happened."

Calvin nodded slowly. "Good idea. And I'll search around in the antique books in the store for any old maps or records that could show ley lines converging around here."

The stones pinged loudly against the sides of the box, jumping higher now.

Luke let out a low whistle. "Seems like these stones are listening. I can see if there is anything in the government archives. Dorian knows the epicenter is here in Noquitt, so maybe she has something more specific." Luke pulled a piece of paper out of his pocket and turned to Fiona. "I got some vibration frequencies from Dorian, but she had no idea how many stones align."

"Thanks. That will help." Fiona took the paper.

"Specifics about the epicenter would be good. Noquitt is a small town, but it will still be like looking for a needle in a haystack unless we have more to go on," Morgan said, not taking her eyes off the bouncing stones. They were leaping higher and higher.

"Yeah. Priority one is finding where this epicenter is, and then we need to figure out what to do about it."

No sooner were the words out of Fiona's mouth than the stones shot out toward the window, where they pinged against the glass and fell to the floor. Belladonna was on them in a second, batting them around and chasing them as they whirled and hit the window over and over.

"That's odd," Fiona said.

"And annoying." Celeste put her hands over her ears.

"I hope they don't break the window," Johanna said as she tried to grab the unwieldy stones.

"They were pinging against the window at Sticks and Stones, almost as if they were trying to get out." Fiona gazed out the window. "And look how they are only going for one window. I believe that is the same direction that they were heading at the store."

Morgan glanced out. Just outside the window was the row of herbs that were having an unusual growth spurt, and beyond that was the section of forest that she had seen Belladonna disappear into. "I think I know where the center of the alignment is."

CHAPTER 9

"*I* think the stones *are* trying to tell us something!" Morgan said as she tried to catch them. "Earlier, I noticed the herbs in the garden are growing at an unnatural rate, almost vibrating with energy themselves. And I saw Belladonna dart into the woods right near that spot, as if she sensed something there."

Morgan hurried toward the kitchen door, struggling to contain the vibrating stones, which now felt hot in her hands. Everyone shoved away from the table and followed. Luke flung the door open for her, and Morgan ran outside.

The stones grew even more energetic, pulsating with heat. "I think the center of the ley line alignment must be somewhere in those woods. These stones are being drawn there for some reason. I can feel it."

The stones throbbed urgently in Morgan's hands as if affirming her words. They pinged against her skin, which stung. "Ouch!"

The stones shot out of her hands and hurled straight into the woods.

"Meow!" Belladonna shot toward the woods after the stones, pausing only for a quick second at the very edge to look back.

"I think she wants us to follow," Jolene said.

The hairs on Morgan's arms prickled as they got closer to the woods. The trees here seemed to lean closer together, blocking out more of the afternoon sun and casting dark shadows across their path. The air felt heavy, and Morgan noticed the others becoming more alert as they moved deeper into the forest.

Celeste paused, tilting her head as if listening. "Can you feel that?" she asked. "It's like a hum... a vibration."

Fiona nodded, her brow furrowed in concentration. "It's getting stronger the farther in we go."

Morgan reached out with her senses, probing the currents of magical energy that flowed through this place. The humming vibration Celeste had described thrummed against her psychic touch. It was chaotic, swirling with an almost angry intensity.

She glanced back at Jolene and Mateo. It seemed they could detect the disturbance too. Jolene rolled her amulet between her fingers, her eyes vigilant. Mateo scanned the woods, one hand resting lightly near his hip.

Fiona had picked up some rocks and was walking cautiously, staying close to Jake.

"I feel like we are on the right track," Morgan said. She quickened her steps, following the faint trail left by the bouncing stones. The air seemed to crackle with power now. Her skin prickled where dark magic roiled just out of sight.

"Y'all getting creeped out too?" Celeste asked, glancing back at the others.

Jolene rolled her amulet between her fingers, eyes scanning the woods. "This place gives me the heebie-jeebies something fierce."

"No kidding. Even the animals are acting weird." Mateo gestured toward the top of a pine tree, where a blue jay hung upside down on a branch above them, blinking and swiveling its head unnaturally as they passed.

Fiona edged closer to Jake. "This is like something out of *The Blair Witch Project*."

Jake nodded, lips pressed into a grim line. "Stay close. I have a bad feeling."

The group moved closer together and slowed their pace, wary of the shadows in the woods. If this assignment was like their others, they could be attacked at any moment.

A rustle in the leaves had them all pivoting toward the noise, ready to fight.

Morgan relaxed when she saw it was just a rabbit.

"Aww... a bunny," Jolene said as the furry brown creature hopped up to them.

"Weird behavior," Mateo said.

The bunny looked up at him, flicked his pink ears, and then hopped onto Cal's boot.

"Very weird." Cal reached down and gently pushed it off.

"Glad it didn't turn into a killer rabbit," Jake said.

The bunny simply stood there blinking at them.

They kept moving through the woods, leaves and twigs crunching under their feet. The air hummed louder. Morgan sensed they were very close to the focal point of the strange energy that had drawn them there.

"Is it getting darker in here?" Fiona asked.

"And creepier," Celeste added.

Morgan stopped short. "Did you see that? Something moved behind that tree."

Morgan's heart pounded as she pressed her back against her sisters, ready to face whatever emerged from the shadows. An ominous laugh echoed through the trees, raising the hairs on her neck. She peered into the gloom, searching for the source. A flicker of movement caught her eye—a flash of green darting behind a broad oak.

"Over there!" Morgan pointed, her voice sharp. In sync, the four sisters pivoted, magic crackling at their fingertips as they turned to face the potential threat.

Mateo's stance widened, ready to charge or defend. "Someone's here," he confirmed grimly. He crouched into a battle stance.

Another dark chuckle rolled through the trees, closer this time. The shadows seemed to stretch and swirl at the edges of their vision. Morgan's breath quickened, and her palms grew slick with sweat. She reached out again with her senses, probing the area psychically even as her eyes darted about. There—a human-sized void, an empty spot where no life energy emanated.

"I don't sense a human presence," Morgan said, her voice low. "But there's something there."

"Something dark," Fiona added with a shiver.

Jolene clutched her amulet, the obsidian warm in her fist. Jake and Cal shifted closer to the sisters protectively.

Morgan saw it again—a flash of emerald green swooping between the trees. Was that a cloak? She pointed, ready to give chase, when a wave of dizziness washed over her. The ground seemed to tilt and swirl beneath her feet. She stumbled, thrown off-balance by the sudden vertigo.

Celeste grabbed her arm, steadying her. "You okay?"

Morgan blinked hard, shaking her head to try and clear it. "Dizzy... like the whole forest is spinning."

"It's this place," said Jolene with a scowl. "All the wild magic—it's messing with our heads."

Morgan blinked hard, trying to shake off the dizziness. A cold wind swept through the trees, sending leaves spiraling up in tiny cyclones. The air crackled with power—she could feel the hairs on her arms standing on end.

Out of the corner of her eye, Morgan saw something move. Her sisters sprang into action beside her. The air filled with light as Fiona sent a volley of glowing orbs arcing toward their attacker. Celeste drew intricate symbols in the air, chanting under her breath while Jolene thrust her palms up, sending arcs of purple energy outward. Mateo stepped to the side and lobbed some sort of power ball at the shadow.

Morgan grabbed Fiona and Celeste's hands, linking their power. Together, the sisters summoned a blinding flash of light, momentarily dispelling the shadows. They heard an otherworldly shriek.

Seizing the opportunity, Jolene lunged forward. "Begone!" she cried, sending out a volley of energy streams.

The shadow jumped out from behind the tree and sent a streak of black energy in retaliation. Morgan deflected it with her amulet, sending it back toward the attacker.

With an unearthly wail, the dark shadow dissolved into smoke before their eyes.

"Is it gone?" Cal asked, peeking out from behind Celeste.

"I think so." Jolene walked slowly toward the pile of ash.

Morgan held her breath, expecting the ash to rise up and attack, but it didn't. "The energy here seems to be getting less heavy."

Her sisters nodded. They all glanced around, still wary, but the forest had grown strangely silent.

"Well, we sure showed *it* who's boss," said Jolene.

She rubbed her palms together then turned to her sisters. "Good teamwork, guys."

Mateo cleared his throat, and Jolene grabbed his hand. "You, too, of course."

Morgan was still on edge after the confrontation with the shadowy being. "Did anyone see the swirl of a green cloak?" she asked. "I only caught glimpses as they darted between the trees."

The others shook their heads.

"Do you think it was the woman who came into the shop?" Fiona frowned. "She certainly was mysterious."

Jake nodded slowly. "If it was her, do you think she was controlling that shadow creature? Trying to attack us?"

Morgan bit her lip, considering. The flashes of green she'd seen had seemed more like someone trying to flee than someone trying to orchestrate an assault. "I don't know. It almost seemed like she was running from it, not working with it."

Celeste crossed her arms, gazing back at the ashes. "If that lady summoned something nasty, it could have turned on her. Messing with forces you don't understand is dangerous business."

"I guess we still have a lot to learn about this," Morgan said. "And even though things seem okay now, I have a feeling this is just the beginning."

"Agreed. We can't let our guard down," Fiona said.

Just then, a white blur sped toward them.

"Belladonna!" Morgan exclaimed as the cat sprinted by, ears flat against her head. A large squirrel with spiky antlers was hot on her heels, chittering angrily.

As Belladonna raced past, Morgan could have sworn she heard the cat's voice in her head, a panicked meow. Run!

Morgan didn't hesitate. "You heard her—let's move!" She took off after Belladonna, trusting her sisters and friends to follow.

"What is that thing?" Fiona yelled from close behind as the antlered squirrel scrambled after Belladonna.

"No clue, but it can't be good!" Morgan vaulted over a fallen log, never taking her eyes off of Belladonna's swishing tail. She could feel the others right on her heels—apparently, they were all eager to get away from this area.

Morgan could see light through the opening in the trees that led to their yard. Belladonna was heading straight for it, and so was the antlered creature. But right before they reached the opening, the creature took a sharp left and veered deeper into the forest.

Morgan burst out into the yard with the others close behind.

Belladonna sat a few feet away, lazily swooshing her tail.

"Belladonna, are you okay?" Morgan ran to the cat, who stretched and flicked her tail as if nothing had happened.

"Okay, that's weird." Fiona picked the cat up and looked her over. "She seems fine. Normal."

Celeste turned to Morgan. "What did you mean when you said, 'You heard her. Run!'"

"Oh, did I say that?" Morgan glanced at Belladonna to see if the cat had anything to say, but all she got was a blank stare. "I thought Belladonna was communicating with me telepathically."

"Cool," Celeste said.

Morgan tensed as their mother rushed out of the house, worry creasing her brow. They had given Johanna strict orders not to engage in any paranormal confrontations for her own safety since Dr. Bly had drained Johanna of her powers. But Morgan knew how hard it was for her mother to sit idly by while her daughters faced danger.

"Are you girls all right?" Johanna asked anxiously, looking them over for any signs of injury.

"We're okay, Mom," Morgan said.

"What happened?" Johanna ushered them all inside and locked the door behind them.

As Johanna bustled about the kitchen brewing tea, Morgan and her sisters recounted the strange events in the forest—the oppressive atmosphere, the swirling shadows, the attack by the cloaked being.

"We didn't find the actual epicenter," Morgan explained, "but it's somewhere in those woods. The magical energy is so intense there." She shuddered at the memory.

Morgan jumped at the sudden ringing of the doorbell, her heart pounding as she exchanged wary looks with her sisters. "I guess I should get that."

Everyone nodded, so Morgan went into the hall, her sisters right behind her.

Peering through the peephole, Morgan saw an elderly man leaning heavily on a gnarled wooden cane on the porch. His wispy white hair stuck out at odd angles from beneath a faded ball cap. Morgan hesitated then cautiously opened the door a crack.

"Good evening," the old man rasped, his voice like sandpaper. "I'm Maynard Dove, and I believe you have something that belongs to me."

CHAPTER 10

Morgan kept the door ajar, peering skeptically at the old man on the porch. "Mr. Dove, what is it that you think we have of yours?"

Maynard Dove's hands clenched around his cane. "The stones," he said. "They were part of my private collection, and I've been informed they found their way to you."

Behind the door, Morgan shared a look with her sisters. Without a word, they understood each other. It was Fiona who stepped up, her voice calm and even. "We have nothing of the sort, Mr. Dove. If you've been robbed, I suggest you talk to the sheriff."

He squinted, betraying a desperate understanding. "Those stones are far more significant than you realize," Dove whispered, the urgency in his voice punctuated by a sudden clap of thunder. "They are key to controlling the effects of the celestial phenomenon. Without them—"

A foreboding rumble interrupted him, and the sky outside darkened unnaturally quickly. The air around them seemed to press closer, the anticipation of the storm mingling with an unseen tension.

Celeste chimed in, her words light yet firm. "It appears we're in for a storm, Mr. Dove. Perhaps this conversation can wait until tomorrow, when it's safe."

Dove, however, stood his ground. "I must insist—"

Raindrops began to fall, tapping hurriedly on the porch. Morgan's intuition told her that they needed to hear Maynard Dove out. Time was of the essence. "All right, come in," she relented. "But we can't promise that we have anything of yours."

It was true. Morgan hadn't seen the stones since they flew into the woods, and she had no idea where they were now. But it was clear the stones were important, and they needed to know what Mr. Dove knew about them. Morgan led the old man toward the kitchen.

His eyes darted around the foyer, lingering on the antique portraits of their ancestors that lined the wall. She thought she saw a glimmer of recognition in his gaze, as if he knew some of the faces staring back at him. But that was impossible; those people had been dead for a hundred years or more.

Johanna busied herself preparing a pot of chamomile tea, gently insisting that Mr. Dove have a cup to warm himself from the damp outside. He acquiesced with a polite nod and settled into one of the wooden chairs at the table as rain pelted the window.

Morgan watched the old man carefully as he sipped the tea. At first glance, he seemed like a harmless old guy, frail and dependent on his cane. But Morgan knew better than to make assumptions based on appearances alone. In her experience, the paranormal world was often deceptive.

"Now, Mr. Dove, why don't you tell us exactly what you are looking for?" Fiona asked.

Maynard Dove fixed his piercing gaze on her. "You must be Fiona," he said. "I think you know exactly what it is. I'm not here to harm any of you, and there is no need to play games."

Fiona met his stare, her jaw tightening. "Mr. Dove, I assure you we are not playing games. I think *you* might be, though. Why can't you just come out and tell us what you're looking for so we can help you?"

Dove's eyes narrowed, his wrinkled face creasing

further. "The stones," he stated plainly. "The ones that move and vibrate of their own accord. I know they came into your possession recently."

Fiona glanced at Morgan, who nodded. They might as well get it out in the open if they were going to find any answers.

Fiona sighed. "Yes, I know the stones you're talking about. But we didn't steal them from you."

"I know that," Dove said. "But I would like them back."

"I'm afraid that won't be possible," Morgan said.

Dove's face darkened. "Why not?"

Morgan looked out the kitchen window toward the woods. "They flew off into the woods, and we haven't seen them since."

Dove studied Morgan as if trying to ascertain whether she spoke the truth. After a moment, he sighed, his shoulders slumping slightly.

"This is... unfortunate," he said. "Without those stones, I fear events will unfold that cannot be easily undone." His voice took on a grave quality that sent a chill down Morgan's spine.

Morgan studied their guest, noting the concern in his eyes. "Mr. Dove, it's clear you know something important about those stones. What, exactly, will happen without them?"

Dove hesitated, his fingers tapping on the handle of his cane. "It's... complicated," he said after a moment. "I'm not sure you would understand."

Morgan glanced at her sisters. They all gave slight nods, communicating without words.

"Mr. Dove," Morgan said gently, "I think you'll find we understand more than you realize. We know about the upcoming celestial alignment and the effect it could have."

Dove nodded as if he wasn't surprised at what they knew. He studied Morgan carefully. "How do you know about that?"

Morgan met his gaze evenly. "Let's just say we have our sources. We also have reason to believe whatever is happening is focused around the woods bordering our property, where the stones disappeared."

Dove leaned back in his chair, regarding the sisters thoughtfully. "I thought you might know more than you let on," he said finally. "Very well. I will tell you what I know if you share what you have learned. Our knowledge together may shed some light on the situation."

Morgan nodded. "Agreed." She could tell Dove still had his guard up, but she sensed he was telling the truth. They were at an impasse, and both had information the other needed. She still wasn't sure if she could trust him, but it made sense to at least hear him out.

"You first," she prompted. "What will happen without those stones?"

Dove took a deep breath as if mentally preparing to unload a heavy burden he had carried alone for too long.

Morgan leaned forward, listening intently as Maynard Dove began his tale.

"Those stones amplify magical power," he said gravely. "And they are drawn to the epicenter of mystical energy, wherever that may be. In this case, it seems they have been pulled into the woods near your home." He paused, taking a slow sip of tea before continuing. "When the celestial alignment occurs, the stones will cluster at the focal point, amplifying the supernatural effects exponentially."

Jolene furrowed her brow, skepticism written on her face. "How do we know you're telling the truth?" she asked pointedly. "Why should we believe anything you say?"

Dove regarded her calmly. "You have no reason to trust me yet," he acknowledged. "But I am not your enemy, nor am I the cause of the strange events occurring. I only wish to contain the damage."

He set down his teacup with a clink. "Let me start

from the beginning. I am a wizard of old—my sister and I were once very powerful practitioners of the arcane arts. But we had a terrible falling out centuries ago and have become estranged."

His eyes took on a faraway look as if peering into the distant past. "This celestial alignment holds special significance for us. We once stopped an alignment from wreaking havoc together, but now, I am afraid my sister wants the opposite effect. That is why it is imperative I recover those stones before they cause damage."

Dove refocused his gaze on the sisters, his expression grave. "Make no mistake, the magic unleashed will be chaotic and dangerous if the stones are allowed to run unchecked. I only wish to mitigate the effects."

He spread his hands imploringly. "I know you have no reason to trust me. But I beg you to believe that I mean you no harm. We must work together if there is to be any hope of controlling the impending supernatural storm." The old wizard fell silent, awaiting the sisters' response.

Morgan weighed his words carefully. She sensed no deceit, only earnest concern.

"Very well," Morgan said finally. "We will take you at your word... for now. But know that we will be watching closely." She glanced at her sisters and saw her own resolve mirrored in their eyes.

Dove inclined his head gratefully. "That is all I ask. With your help, perhaps we can prevent a catastrophe."

The rain continued to patter steadily on the window as Morgan told Dove about their foray into the forest.

"I'm afraid strange things are already happening," Fiona said. "We encountered odd animal behavior and strange creatures."

"And something tried to attack us," Celeste added.

"Attack you?" Dove seemed unsettled. "Did you see them?"

Jolene folded her arms across her chest, a skeptical look on her face. "We didn't get a good look at whatever it was that attacked us," she explained matter-of-factly. "It was more like a dark, shadowy figure."

Dove raised an eyebrow. "Just one? That seems... odd." He tapped his cane thoughtfully.

Luke piped up from where he was leaning against the kitchen counter. "There was something else in those woods too," he said. "I only caught a glimpse, but it looked like someone in a green cape. Whoever it was turned and ran off when they saw us coming."

At the mention of the green cape, Dove's expression turned grave. "Green cape, you say?" His voice was tight.

Luke nodded. "Yep, emerald green."

Dove's knuckles whitened as he tightened his grip on his cane. "That was my sister, Sofie," he said, urgency creeping into his tone. "You must avoid her at all costs. She is unpredictable right now. And very dangerous."

CHAPTER 11

"Do you think we can trust him?" Morgan asked after Dove left.

Jolene shook her head skeptically. "You know the first rule. Never trust anyone but ourselves until we have solid proof they are trustworthy."

At that moment, Belladonna trotted into the room, her tail held high. She went straight to Celeste, rubbing against her leg with a loud purr.

"Where did you come from?" Celeste bent down to scratch the cat's ears. "Kind of weird that she wasn't here when Dove was in the house. Now she just happens to show up as soon as he leaves?"

Johanna tilted her head to study the cat. "Sometimes, she can be shy. She's famous for sneaking off to one of her many hiding spots for a nap. Could be just a coincidence."

Jake nodded slowly, arms crossed, as he pondered their dilemma. "Maybe so, but we can't ignore our instincts. Something feels off about Dove's story. We need to be cautious until we know more."

"Agreed," Cal said. "He tried to warn us about Sofie, but for all we know, his sister in the green cape is the good guy and Dove is the bad guy."

"I don't know about that," Fiona said. "If it's the woman in the green cape who came into Sticks and Stones, I got a bad vibe from her. Then again, she didn't actually do anything bad. I suppose she was looking for the stones so that she could prevent them from finding their way into the woods."

"Guess we didn't do a very good job at preventing that," Morgan said.

Johanna smiled reassuringly at her daughters. "That's all right. I'm sure we can figure out a way to remedy the situation," she said.

Celeste nodded. "First thing tomorrow, I'll start trying to conjure up some ghosts from among our ancestors. They may be able to provide some insight into all this."

Luke chimed in, "I'll contact Dorian tonight to see

if she has any additional information that could help and find out exactly when this alignment is."

Calvin added, "I can dig into some old maps of the area to see if they indicate anything about ley lines or past strange occurrences."

Mateo piped up, "Oh, and I know someone we can talk to about ley lines and alignments. She's kind of an expert on these sorts of things. Jolene, want to come with me to meet her tomorrow?"

Jolene smiled. "Sure, that sounds great. The more we can learn about what's really going on here, the better."

"Hey, look, it's not raining anymore." Celeste pointed at the window.

Outside, the rain had stopped, and sunshine was breaking through the clouds. Morgan's gaze drifted to the woods. Despite the sunshine, they were still dark and ominous. "Did you guys notice that the darkest energy seemed to be deeper into the woods?"

"Meow!" Belladonna hopped up into the windowsill and looked out toward the woods with the rest of them.

"I did, and that crazy squirrel-elope thing didn't follow us out as if it didn't want to leave the woods," Fiona said.

"Nothing dangerous followed us out, which is good," Mateo added.

"Yeah." Celeste looked out at the woods too. "Good thing whatever weirdness is in there isn't spilling out into our yard."

"At least not yet," Fiona said grimly.

CHAPTER 12

Celeste loved the library in the morning. The sunlight slanted in through the windows on the eastern side, and the morning light illuminated the Oriental rug, intensifying its colors. It smelled good, too, like vanilla, paper, and leather.

She sat on the floor and lit the candles with a practiced hand, murmuring an incantation under her breath. The sage smoldered, wisps of smoke curling into the air. She focused her energy, visualizing the spirits she hoped to summon. The candles flickered, shadows dancing across the walls of the old library.

Celeste closed her eyes and focused, sending a telepathic call out into the ether. "Calling all ghosts from the fifteen hundreds. I'm summoning you to the library this morning. We've got candles, we've got sage —it's a happening scene. Show up, and let's chat."

She waited, listening intently. A few wispy responses fluttered by, as indistinct as static on the radio. But no ghosts materialized.

Celeste huffed in frustration. "C'mon, don't leave a girl hanging. I know you're out there." She visualized the spirits, imagining their old-timey clothes and accents. "Verily, methinks thou art most cordially invited to convene posthaste."

A cold breeze suddenly gusted through the room, extinguishing the candles. Celeste shivered, goose bumps rising on her arms.

"Who's there?" she called out.

The ghostly form of Rebekah materialized before her.

"Hi, Rebekah." Celeste tried to hide her disappointment.

"What, I'm not good enough?" Rebekah said, a sarcastic lilt to her voice. "You sent out a summoning signal."

"I need information about the last major celestial alignment, which was five hundred years ago," Celeste explained. "I was hoping to speak with someone from that time."

"Oh, I'm not nearly that old." Rebekah sighed. "But maybe what you seek is closer than you realize."

Celeste made a face. It was just like Rebekah to talk in riddles.

Rebekah's ghostly figure flickered, growing fainter. "I'll just go back to my work, then."

Rebekah drifted back to the odd brass contraption in the corner, the thing that looked like a mash-up of binoculars and a sextant. She peered through it intently, as if looking for something just out of sight, right before she disappeared totally.

Celeste sighed. Another dead end. She tried for a few minutes more, but she'd used up all her ghost-conjuring energy. She blew out the candles and began gathering up her materials.

The library doors creaked open, and Morgan and Fiona peeked in.

"Any luck reaching the great beyond?" Morgan asked.

"None," Celeste huffed. "I couldn't get any ghosts that were around back during the last alignment."

"Don't worry," Morgan said. "We know you'll be able to get to them. Fiona and I are heading to Sticks and Stones to make some protective crystals and herbs before we go back into the woods."

Celeste managed a smile. "Good idea. I'm going to take a break then will be back at it later on."

The sound of crickets chirping blared into the room.

"Your phone's ringing again," Morgan said, nudging Fiona with her elbow.

Fiona fished the phone out of her pocket. "It's Jake," she said before answering with a bright, "Hey, you."

Morgan and Celeste exchanged knowing looks as Fiona nodded along, murmuring "uh-huhs" and "okays."

"Be careful," Fiona said finally, hanging up.

"What's he up to?" Morgan asked.

"He's going to the jail to talk to that Alex Summers who pawned the stones. Sheriff White isn't coming in until later, so one of his buddies is letting him in."

Celeste nudged Fiona with her elbow. "Jake calls a lot. He's got you on a short leash, doesn't he?"

Fiona rolled her eyes. "He's just looking out for me."

"Uh-huh, sure," Celeste teased.

Before Fiona could respond, Celeste's phone buzzed in her pocket. She glanced at the screen, and a faint blush rose on her cheeks.

"Who's that? Cal?" Fiona asked, a knowing grin spreading across her face.

"Maybe," Celeste mumbled, answering it. "Hi, Cal."

"Thought so," Fiona said. "Don't dish it out if you can't take it."

Celeste simply smiled and waved goodbye to her sisters as they headed toward the front door.

"How's my favorite ghost whisperer?" Cal asked.

Celeste rolled her eyes. "Not great. I tried to make contact with a ghost from five hundred years ago but came up empty."

"Sorry to hear that," Cal said. "But hey, you can't force these things. Why don't you swing by the antique store around noon? I'll have a chipotle chicken rice bowl with avocado from Fresh waiting for you."

"Ooh, you know just how to lift my spirits," Celeste said, smiling. "It's a date. See you soon!" She ended the call, her mood brightening at the thought of spending the afternoon with Cal.

CHAPTER 13

Jake glanced around the lobby of the Noquitt police station just to be sure Sheriff White wasn't there. It was quiet. The linoleum floor tiles gleamed, and the plastic chairs sat unoccupied.

Debra looked up from behind the reception desk. In front of her sat a Styrofoam cup of coffee and a half-eaten glazed donut. "She's not in. It's a great break."

Jake laughed. "I'll bet it is. I'm not here to see the sheriff, though. Is Tony in?"

Jake was grateful that he'd kept his old connections on the force. They sure came in handy when he needed favors. Tony had been happy to arrange for Jake to talk to Alex Summers in his jail cell. Sending a dozen donuts over this morning hadn't hurt either.

"He sure is." Debra turned her head toward the back and bellowed, "Tony!"

A burly man with a bushy mustache appeared from the back, wiping donut powder from his uniform pants.

"Jake! Good to see you," Tony said, giving Jake a hearty handshake. "Let's head on back before her highness comes back in. You've got about an hour."

Jake nodded, falling into step beside Tony as they made their way past the front desk. Debra glanced up, curiosity glinting in her eyes.

"Mum's the word, Debra," Tony said with a wink.

"My lips are zipped," Debra replied, making a locking motion over her mouth before returning her attention to the computer screen.

Jake was grateful for the discretion. The last thing he needed was to have Sheriff White questioning why he wanted to talk to Alex Summers. White didn't trust Jake, and she knew nothing about paranormal happenings.

Tony led Jake down the familiar concrete hallway to the small jail area, home to only three cells. Though Jake had walked this path many times as a deputy, it felt different being on the outside now.

Alex Summers lay sprawled on the cot in the first cell, one leg dangling off the edge. The cell was a dingy gray, with a steel toilet-and-sink combo that had seen better days. Alex squinted at Jake through the bars, his greasy blond hair falling into his eyes.

"What do you want?" Alex grumbled, sitting up and swinging his other leg over the side of the cot. His posture was defensive, his shoulders hunched.

Jake folded his arms and leaned against the concrete wall outside Alex's cell. "I've got some questions for you," he said casually.

Alex scoffed, not making eye contact. "Yeah, get in line, buddy."

"It's about some stones that went missing. Special stones belonging to a man named Maynard Dove."

At the mention of the stones, Alex sat up straight and turned his full attention to Jake. His nonchalant attitude vanished. "What do you know about those stones?" Alex asked sharply.

"Just that they're important. Very important." Jake looked at Alex. "And that you and Dove have some history."

Alex shook his head, cursing under his breath. He stood and began pacing the short length of the cell.

"That old fool. He'll ruin everything if he gets those stones back," Alex muttered. He wheeled around to face Jake. "Yeah, I took the stones, okay? But not to sell them. I did it to protect them."

Jake raised an eyebrow. "Protect them from what?"

Alex gripped the bars, his knuckles white. "Do you know the significance of those stones?"

Jake nodded. "I do."

"I was protecting them from Dove. He has no idea the kind of power he's messing with."

Jake regarded Alex skeptically. "If Dove is so dangerous, why'd you work for him in the first place?"

Alex ran a hand through his greasy hair. "It's complicated. Dove's not a bad guy, exactly. He wants to stop chaos from happening. But his methods are risky. He thinks he can force the energy, but not everything works like that."

Jake's skepticism remained. "So you stole the stones to what, save the world?"

"I stole them to get them away from Dove before he does something stupid," Alex shot back. "Energy needs to be finessed in a certain way, but Dove insists on forcing things."

Jake looked at Alex skeptically. "All right, so if you wanted to protect these special stones so badly, why'd you pawn them? Seems kind of dumb if you were trying to keep them safe."

Alex's eyes darted around the cell, avoiding Jake's gaze. He fidgeted nervously with his hands. "Well, uh, I had to make it look convincing, you know? Like I was just some thief pawning random stuff. I figured if I stole a bunch of things from Dove's place, not just the stones, the cops would be too busy tracking down all the other missing items to realize the stones were important."

Jake raised an eyebrow, still not entirely convinced. "But if you pawned the stones, how would you know where they ended up?"

Alex got more nervous. "Well, anywhere would be better than with Dove. He's trying to force the ley lines, and that won't bode well for the celestial alignment."

Before Jake could say anything else, Sheriff White's sharp voice cut in from behind Jake. "Ley lines? Celestial alignments? What kind of nonsense are you two talking about?"

Jake whirled around to see Sheriff White standing there with her arms crossed, an irritated expression on her face. His heart sank. This was not good.

Jake's mind raced as he blurted an excuse to Sheriff White. "I have no idea what he's talking about. Maybe he's practicing for an insanity plea," he said, the laugh that followed sounding hollow even to his own ears.

Sheriff White advanced, a mix of suspicion and

curiosity hardening her features. "What are you doing here, Cooper?" she demanded.

Shuffling backward with feigned ease, Jake replied, "I needed to chat with Summers about a case."

Her eyes narrowed like the barrel of a gun zeroing in on a target. "And what case would that be?"

Jake dodged the question with practiced vagueness. "It's connected to Reed Antiques," he said, the casual shrug of his shoulders belying the tension coiling within.

A silent accusation hung in the air as White's stony gaze drilled into him. "That's where your friend does business, right? The place receiving stolen property?"

"Absolutely," Jake agreed, injecting lightness into his voice that felt like lifting a too-heavy weight. "And what's wrong with mixing business with friendship?" His laughter rang false in the cold air of the station.

"I've got to run. Heavy day and all," he tossed out, sidling toward the door. He turned his back on White and tried not to break into a run. "Always a pleasure, Sheriff," he called out over his shoulder, not waiting for her reply.

Jake strode briskly down Main Street, hands shoved into his pockets, thoughts churning. His conversation with Alex Summers had left him with more questions than answers. Summers definitely knew those stones were important, but the guy was obviously hiding something. Why steal the stones just to pawn them? It didn't add up.

Jake reached the brick building that housed his office and headed up the stairs. He could hear Jolene's voice from out in the hallway, punctuated by Mateo's deep rumble. Jake opened the door to find Jolene perched on the edge of the desk, swinging her legs, while Mateo leaned against the wall.

"Hey, you two. What's up?" Jake asked.

"Hey." Jolene hopped down. "We're going to talk to one of Mateo's paranormal contacts, see if they have any intel about the celestial alignment."

Jake nodded. "Good thinking. I just came from the station, where I had a chat with Alex Summers."

Mateo's dark eyebrows shot up. "The guy who stole the stones? What did he have to say?"

"Claims he took them to protect them from Maynard Dove. He seems to think Maynard might be about to do something harmful." Jake shook his head. "Not sure I buy it, though. Something's off with his story."

Jolene tugged thoughtfully on a strand of brown hair. "Protecting them makes sense, I guess, but why steal them at all, then?"

"Exactly," Jake said. "Anyway, I'll dig into it. You

guys want to meet up at the house later? We can compare notes."

Mateo pushed off from the wall. "Sounds good. Be careful, Jake. We still don't know who we can trust."

Jake clapped Mateo on the shoulder. "You too. See you tonight."

CHAPTER 14

Mateo squeezed Jolene's hand tightly as they walked briskly down the dimly lit side street. His eyes continuously scanned their surroundings, alert for any sign of a tail.

"Remember, this place is secret for a reason," he said in a hushed tone. "We can't tell anyone the location. Not even your sisters."

Jolene nodded, lips pressed together. Mateo led her through a decrepit brick building to a flaking green door. He rapped three times in quick succession, then uttered a phrase in Latin she didn't quite catch.

The door creaked open, and they slipped inside. Jolene blinked, eyes adjusting to the dark interior.

Mateo led Jolene down the dank underground tunnel, his footsteps echoing off the cold stone walls.

"Creepy down here," Jolene muttered, peering into the darkness ahead.

Mateo flashed a grin. "Scared?"

"You wish," she scoffed.

They walked in silence for several minutes, the only sounds being their footsteps and the occasional skittering of unseen creatures. Jolene jumped as a loud screech reverberated through the passage.

"What was that?" she whispered.

"Probably just some bats," Mateo said. But he scanned the shadows warily.

After a few more twists and turns, they arrived at a heavy wooden door reinforced with iron bands. Again, Mateo rapped three times in quick succession then uttered, "*Aperi ianuam.*"

The door creaked open slowly, spilling dim golden light into the passageway. Jolene peered inside curiously, squinting as her eyes adjusted.

The seedy bar's long, narrow interior stretched into the distance. Dark wood covered every surface, aged to a burnished patina from centuries of use. A lonely bartender in a red vest endlessly polished a beer glass behind the counter. He nodded almost imperceptibly at their entrance.

Mateo led Jolene to a corner booth tucked into the shadows. She slid onto the cracked leather seat, senses heightened. Her eyes darted around, taking in the odd assortment of characters occupying the other booths. She leaned in close to Mateo. "What is this place?" she whispered.

Mateo's eyes crinkled with amusement. "Let's just say it caters to a very unique clientele. But it's safe. I promise."

He waved to the bartender, who brought over two glasses of cloudy amber liquid. Jolene took a cautious sip, feeling the mysterious establishment's secrets swirling around her in the gloom as the drink's smoky sweetness warmed her insides.

A woman with waist-length raven hair sauntered over to their booth. Her bloodred lips curled into a knowing smile as she slid in across from them. "Mateo. It's been too long," she purred in a husky voice.

Mateo nodded in greeting. "Jolene, meet Astrid Nightwhisper. She's an old friend with a knack for gathering useful information."

Astrid's dark eyes gleamed as she turned her gaze on Jolene. "Charmed, I'm sure."

Jolene shifted uncomfortably under the intensity of Astrid's stare. There was something not quite human about the woman that set Jolene's senses tingling.

Mateo got right to business. "We're here because

strange things are happening back home. Unnatural occurrences in the woods, disturbances in the magical currents. We were hoping you might have some insight."

Astrid leaned back, absently stirring her bright-blue drink with one long red fingernail. A spire of smoke wafted up out of the glass. "Yes, word travels fast in our circles about the coming alignment. Powerful forces are in motion, and your quaint little town finds itself at the center." She arched one eyebrow. "Tread carefully, darling. The shadows hold many secrets, and not all wish you well."

"What can we do to stop it?" Jolene asked.

Astrid leaned back and studied Jolene. "There are some magical stones. They may be in the hands of an enemy. You will have to find them and mute their powers before the alignment happens."

Jolene glanced at Mateo. "Magical stones? Like crystals that jump around and fly?"

Astrid's eyes widened. "You have them?"

Jolene looked down at her drink. "We had them, but they flew off into the woods."

Astrid let out an exaggerated sigh, rolling her dark-lined eyes. "Amateurs," she muttered and took a long draw from her smoking drink.

Jolene bristled. She did not appreciate being

talked down to by this pretentious woman. She was just about to open her mouth to tell her off when Mateo gave her hand a squeeze. She looked at him, and he shook his head subtly. They needed Astrid's help, and getting on her bad side wouldn't be smart. Jolene bit her tongue.

"Can you tell us anything about these stones?" Mateo asked evenly. "We could use some guidance on how to handle their power."

Leaning back in the booth, Astrid tapped one long, ruby-red nail on the tabletop. "Those stones amplify magical energies tremendously. Without them contained, you're looking at a catastrophic paranormal event when the alignment peaks."

Jolene and Mateo exchanged alarmed glances. This was worse than they had anticipated.

"The ideal scenario would have been to neutralize the stones before the alignment," Astrid continued. "But now, you'll have to deal with them at the focal point. And it won't be pretty."

She leaned across the table, fixing them with an intense stare. "You need a three-tiered magical solution—sticks, stones, and spells. Layer your defenses. Anything less won't withstand the forces you're dealing with."

Jolene met Astrid's gaze unflinchingly. "Looks like

we've got our work cut out for us. But we're used to challenges."

Astrid's red lips quirked upward. "I hope so, darling. Or your quaint little town may not be so charming after this alignment runs its course." She downed the last of her drink in one long swallow then slid gracefully out of the booth. With a parting wink at Mateo, she disappeared into the hazy darkness of the bar.

Jolene let out a breath. "Well, she was cheerful," she muttered sarcastically.

Mateo laughed. "Astrid likes to dramatize. But she knows her stuff." He grew serious. "If she says we need three-tiered defenses, we should listen."

Jolene nodded slowly, wondering if she could trust Astrid. She didn't like the way she'd winked at Mateo. But was that just because she was jealous?

Jolene swirled the remnants of her smoky drink, avoiding Mateo's gaze. She knew she shouldn't ask, but the question slipped out before she could stop herself. "So... how do you know Astrid exactly?"

Mateo laughed, his eyes crinkling at the corners. "We go way back, but nothing romantic if that's what you're worried about."

Jolene felt her cheeks flush, but Mateo's words rang true. She decided to change the subject.

"Anyway, we should talk about Astrid's warning. She mentioned a three-tiered magical solution using sticks, stones, and spells. I assume the sticks refer to herbs, the stones to crystals."

Mateo nodded, leaning forward with his elbows on the table. "You're right. That's the pressing issue here. Clearly, we need some serious magical firepower to contain those stones when the alignment peaks."

Jolene nodded thoughtfully. "It's a good thing Morgan is so skilled with herbs, Fiona with stones, and Celeste with spells."

Mateo made a face at the mention of Celeste and spells.

Jolene laughed. "Okay, Celeste is fairly decent with spells. She's still learning."

Mateo chuckled. "I'm sure Celeste can rise to the occasion, especially with stakes this high."

Jolene pulled out her cell phone, intending to message her sisters right away about everything they had learned from Astrid. But when she woke up the screen, it was completely blank.

"Ugh, no service," she muttered, waving her phone around, trying in vain to get a signal.

"There's no reception down here," Mateo said apologetically. "Too many things blocking the signals."

Jolene sighed in frustration and slipped her

useless phone back into her pocket. "Then let's get out of this musty old bat cave. I need to tell Celeste, Morgan, and Fiona everything we found out as soon as possible. If Astrid is right, we have a major magical disaster to prevent once that alignment hits."

Mateo nodded gravely as he slid out of the booth. "You're absolutely right. There's no time to waste." He helped Jolene out of her seat. "Let's get back above ground so you can call your sisters. We've got a lot of work to do."

Jolene followed Mateo back through the seedy underground bar, giving the lurking patrons suspicious glances as she passed. She quickened her pace once they were in the dank stone passage, eager to leave this place behind. Their footsteps echoed rapidly as they retraced their path through the winding tunnel.

Jolene breathed a sigh of relief when they stepped out into the cool night air. She immediately pulled out her phone again, relieved to see full signal bars. Her thumbs flew as she typed out a group message to her sisters.

Met a contact of Mateo's named Astrid. She confirmed the magical stones are dangerous. The contact said we need herbs, crystals, and spells to get to and contain them when the alignment peaks. Let's gather everyone for supper tonight. Someone get takeout.

"I sent them a message. We'll meet tonight for supper." Jolene stuffed the phone into her back pocket.

"Sounds good. Who's going to bring takeout?"

CHAPTER 15

"Sounds like Mateo and Jolene made some headway." Morgan held her phone up toward Fiona, who was busy putting together a collection of frequency-muting stones based on the information Luke had gotten from Dorian.

Fiona squinted over at Morgan. "What did she say?"

"They met with a contact of Mateo's, and I guess we'll need a combination of herbs, crystals, and spells to mitigate the effects of the alignment."

"Sounds right up our alley." Fiona held up a small burlap bag and dropped the stones in. "Hopefully, these will be the crystals."

Morgan continued grinding white sage and rosemary with the mortar and pestle, the herbs' pungent aromas filling the air. She tipped the finely crushed mixture into small glass bottles and added a splash of rosewater to each, creating a protective spritzer for their impending foray into the woods.

She held the bottle to the light. "And hopefully, these are the herbs. I hope this is potent enough to shield us from whatever is in the woods."

Fiona nodded. "What about the spells?"

"Good question. Hopefully, Celeste will figure that part out."

Before Fiona could respond, the door burst open. A gust of wind swirled into the cottage, fluttering loose papers and curtains. Framed in the doorway stood a woman draped in an emerald-green cape. Long silver hair spilled over her shoulders, partially obscuring a sharp, angular face. Her piercing gaze fixed on Morgan and Fiona.

Fiona gasped. "You! You were here before."

The woman inclined her head. "Yes. I'm sorry I couldn't be more straightforward when last we met, but I didn't want to fully reveal myself then." Her voice was smooth yet powerful. "I was searching for the stones, you see, in hopes of averting the coming crisis."

Fiona held up her hands defensively. "We don't have the stones."

The woman's icy gaze didn't waver. "I am aware.

Unfortunately, they are more dangerous now than ever."

Morgan straightened her back, eyeing the woman suspiciously. "We know who you are. You're Sofie Dove, aren't you?"

A faint smile curved the woman's lips as she inclined her head. "Indeed, I am."

"Maynard told us about you," Morgan said. "He seemed quite concerned about you causing a disaster in Noquitt."

Sofie let out a low chuckle that was devoid of humor. "Is that so? How ironic." Her gaze met Morgan's squarely. "It's Maynard who poses the real threat."

Fiona crossed her arms over her chest, regarding Sofie with a skeptical look. "Funny you should say that, considering Maynard said the exact same thing about you."

A sigh escaped Sofie's lips, and she looked genuinely tired for a moment. "Yes, I suppose he would," she admitted, her voice heavy with regret. "You see, we both want to control the ley lines—to ensure the paranormal effects of the celestial alignment don't allow entities from the evil realm to escape—but our methods differ greatly."

"How so?" Morgan asked, intrigued despite herself.

"Maynard believes in brute force," Sofie explained, an edge of disdain creeping into her voice. "He wants to bend the ley lines to his will, control them completely. But such power is not meant to be harnessed or controlled—it should be guided and respected."

"And what do you propose?" Fiona asked warily.

Sofie's gaze softened as she looked at each sister in turn. "A more natural approach. One that respects the balance of power and allows the ley lines to align naturally, without interference. It's a more difficult path, certainly, but it's the only way to truly prevent disaster."

Fiona glanced at Morgan, her expression mirroring the confusion and suspicion in her sister's eyes. "How do we know which one of you is right?" she asked, voicing the question they were both thinking.

Sofie smiled, a knowing glint in her eye. "Look to your heart," she advised. "Ask yourself, do you believe in letting nature take its course, or do you believe in attempting to control it?"

"But nature can be unpredictable and dangerous," Morgan argued. "Shouldn't we try to control it if we can?"

Sofie shook her head. "The natural world has its

own balance, its own rhythms. Attempting to control it often leads to more harm than good. You must either dampen the power of the stones or convince Maynard to relinquish his control over the ley lines. Perhaps both."

Fiona frowned. "That's easier said than done."

"I know," Sofie admitted, her gaze growing distant. "But I have faith in you and your sisters. You are far more powerful than you realize."

A sense of urgency crept into Sofie's voice as she continued. "Now that the stones are in the woods, they will seek out the epicenter of the celestial alignment on their own. The energy within the woods will grow increasingly powerful as we approach the alignment. You will need a three-tiered approach—herbs, spells, and crystals."

"And what happens if we can't dampen the stones or stop Maynard?" Morgan asked.

Sofie didn't answer right away, her gaze lingering on each sister as if committing their faces to memory. "Then I fear for Noquitt," she said quietly.

With that, she disappeared as suddenly as she'd arrived, leaving Fiona and Morgan staring at the empty space where she'd been standing moments before.

For a long moment, silence hung heavy in the

room, punctuated only by the soft ticking of an antique clock on the mantel.

"Well," Fiona said at last, breaking the silence, "that was interesting."

Morgan sighed, rubbing her temples as if to ward off an impending headache. "I think I preferred it when our biggest problem was Sheriff White."

"Good thing we are already meeting tonight for supper. Everyone needs to know about this latest development," Fiona said.

Morgan's phone pinged, and she looked at the message. "At least one thing is going well: Celeste is bringing Chinese takeout."

CHAPTER 16

Celeste's phone pinged rapidly as everyone messaged her back with their Chinese food orders. Crab rangoon was always a favorite. Mateo liked veggie fried rice, and Fiona was a coconut shrimp gal. She'd put the order in later.

Celeste tucked her phone back into her pocket. She felt comforted that her whole family would be together tonight, even if it was to discuss the monumental task that lay ahead.

She navigated across the quiet street toward Reed Antiques. As she pushed open the heavy wooden door, a small bell jingled merrily overhead. The familiar scent of old books and polished wood comforted her, momentarily displacing her concerns.

Reed Antiques was an eclectic haven for history

buffs and curiosity seekers. It operated as both a pawn shop and antique store. Dark mahogany shelves lined the walls, groaning under the weight of ancient tomes, ornate trinkets, and faded photographs. Gilded mirrors hung precariously above overstuffed armchairs, reflecting the dim glow of crystal chandeliers suspended from a high ceiling.

Calvin was behind the counter, deep in conversation with a pair of customers. He flashed Celeste a warm smile as she walked in, his eyes sparkling behind the wire-rimmed reading glasses he'd recently started wearing. Celeste returned his smile and meandered through the narrow aisles.

Her fingertips grazed brass statuettes and delicate china figurines, lingering on a set of intricately carved chess pieces. She admired a dusty old gramophone, its brass horn gleaming under the soft light.

The shop was a testament to forgotten times and cherished memories; every item held a story waiting to be discovered. Celeste felt a pang of comfort amid the uncertainty looming over them. As she waited for Cal to finish with his customers, she couldn't help but feel drawn into the hushed whispers of history echoing around her.

Celeste glanced up as Calvin approached, his steps echoing on the hardwood floors.

"Sorry about that," he said, leaning against the counter next to her. "Mr. and Mrs. Elliott like to chat."

Celeste smiled. "No problem. It looked like they were interested in that art nouveau mirror."

Cal nodded. "They're furnishing their lake house. I'm sure I'll be helping them decorate for months." He chuckled softly.

His assistant, Emma, appeared from the back room then, tying an apron around her waist.

"Hey, Celeste," Emma said warmly. "Good to see you."

"You too," Celeste replied.

Calvin straightened up. "Emma's got things covered up here if you want to head downstairs. I pulled out some of the older maps and books that might help us figure things out."

Excitement flickered through Celeste. "Definitely. Lead the way."

Calvin lifted a hinged section of the counter and gestured for Celeste to follow him through a narrow doorway. A steep staircase descended into the basement, lined with framed botanical prints and seashell sconces. Celeste grasped the smooth wooden railing as she carefully made her way down, Calvin a steady presence behind her.

The basement was cool and dim, with exposed

stone walls that gave it an ancient feel. A small desk lamp provided a circle of light amid the shadows. Several large leather-bound books were spread open atop a heavy wooden table alongside unfurled scrolls and yellowed maps weighted down by geodes. Celeste ran her fingers over the cracked spines of the massive tomes, inhaling the comforting vanilla scent of aging paper.

She'd been there before, but each time, she was still filled with awe as her eyes roamed over the array of ancient books and documents. "I can't believe you have all this incredible history right downstairs."

Calvin chuckled. "Perks of owning an antique shop in a town as old as Noquitt." He leaned over the table, tracing his finger along the intricate contours of an ancient map. "I was looking for any references to ley lines, energy channels, sacred sites—anything that might give us a clue."

Celeste followed his gaze. Faded symbols and calligraphic text annotated the map, with odd sketches of stars and symbols in the margins. Her eyes widened as Calvin's finger rested on a point just west of Noquitt.

"See here? There's mention of 'mystical currents' flowing from the forest to the sea. And this symbol indicates a site of power."

Celeste peered closer. "That's so close to our house," she murmured.

Calvin nodded, rolling up his sleeves. "There's more."

He turned the giant pages of one leather-bound book until he reached a chapter titled "The Hidden Forces of New England." Scanning the text, he summarized, "This talks about early settlers sensing strange energies in the wilderness. Some believed the area was a supernatural nexus."

Celeste's pulse quickened. She joined Calvin in examining the books and maps, searching for more clues. After almost an hour, a pattern emerged— multiple sources referencing odd energies corre- sponding to the forest near Blackmoore Manor.

Celeste stared at the ancient maps, her brow furrowed in concentration. Her eyes darted back and forth among the various documents, seeking out any additional clues. The maps had faint dotted lines that all seemed to converge near a stream that ran through the woods west of their home. Could those be the ley lines? She was familiar with that stream, but because of the age of the maps, some of the other landmarks didn't match up with her memory of the area. The precise location of this convergence remained elusive.

Calvin ran his fingers over the parchment, his

expression thoughtful. "I think this is as close as we're going to get for now," he said, tapping on the map where the dotted lines seemed to intersect. "I'm not sure these lines represent the ley lines, but if so, they seem to converge where the stream jogs to the east."

Celeste nodded slowly, taking in the information. They had narrowed it down significantly, but she still felt a pang of frustration at their inability to pinpoint the exact location. She looked down at her hands, stained with ink from tracing over lines and symbols.

They were so close.

"I think you're right," she said finally, lifting her gaze to meet Calvin's.

Just as they began to gather up their materials, a sudden chill ran through Celeste. It was as if a gust of winter wind had swept through the basement, making her shiver uncontrollably. But more than that, it was as if some unseen force was guiding her attention toward something.

She looked up and found herself staring at a brass instrument resting on a nearby shelf. It was tarnished and dusty. And it was also familiar.

Celeste walked to the device and picked it up.

"Cal," she called, her voice echoing slightly in the hushed quiet of the basement. "Look at this."

Calvin looked up from the table and squinted at

her. "I never really figured out what that was. Some kind of old sextant or binocular thing. It's been here for a long time."

"I guess I never noticed it before," she replied. "I saw Rebekah using one just like this when I was communicating with her ghost."

Calvin's eyebrows shot up. "Do you think it could be connected to the alignment?"

Celeste shrugged, turning the instrument over in her hands. "I'm not sure. Rebekah said she knew nothing about the alignment. Her time was hundreds of years later. But every time I've tried to contact a ghost who knows about the last alignment, I get Rebekah, and she is looking through a device that looks exactly like this."

The cold chill had dissipated, but Celeste could still feel a residual tingling sensation in her fingertips as if the sextant was resonating with some kind of latent energy. It had to be connected.

"I think we should bring this to the meeting tonight," Celeste said, her voice filled with conviction. "I think it's meant to help us. This may be the very thing that helps us find the exact location of the epicenter."

CHAPTER 17

"Where is Celeste with the food?" Morgan was starving, and everyone else was already present. She was dying for some crab rangoon and lo mein.

"Just saw her pull in," Jake said as he sat down next to Morgan.

The aroma of fried rice and sweet-and-sour chicken wafted through the Blackmoore kitchen as Celeste set down a couple of large bags on the counter. Morgan perked up instantly. Her stomach rumbled in response to the enticing smells.

"Finally!" Jumping to her feet, she grabbed a pair of chopsticks and began to rummage through the bags, opening the white cardboard containers and setting them on the table so they could pass them around.

They settled down at the table, the kitchen filling with the sounds of clattering chopsticks and muffled conversation. Morgan bit into a crab rangoon, savoring the crunch and the creamy filling. As she swallowed, she caught Luke's eye across the table. His smile was warm, comforting—a silent promise that no matter what happened with this celestial alignment business, they'd face it together.

Morgan cleared her throat, setting aside her food for a moment. "We should probably discuss what we found out today," she said, looking around at her sisters and their respective partners.

Jake nodded, setting down the container of beef and broccoli. "I visited Alex Summers in jail today." He recounted their conversation, mentioning Alex's claim that he'd stolen the stones from Maynard Dove to protect them.

"That sounds like a load of bull," Jolene interjected when Jake finished speaking. "Why would he suddenly develop a conscience?"

Jake shrugged. "That's just what he said, but I felt like he was holding something back."

Mateo then shared his and Jolene's conversation with Astrid Nightwhisper about ley lines and magical stones. Morgan listened, her mind spinning as she tried to make sense of the rapidly unfolding situation.

"That makes sense," she said when Mateo was done. "Fiona and I had a visit from Sofie Dove, and she said something similar about the sticks, stones, and spells."

"Sofie Dove?" Jolene's eyes widened, her forkful of noodles suspended halfway to her mouth. "You're saying she came to visit you two?"

Morgan nodded, reaching for a spring roll. "Yep, green cape and all."

"And she mentioned you need a three-tiered approach?" Mateo asked.

"Yes, and that's not all. She claims that Maynard is the one to watch out for," Fiona said.

Luke made a face. "Sure, that's what Maynard said about her. So who do we believe?"

"Neither." Jake spooned some lo mein out of the carton. "No one can be trusted, as usual."

"I agree," Morgan said. "Sofie also said that she and her brother had different ideas of how to control the lines, and his was going to result in a bad outcome."

Celeste frowned, her blue eyes thoughtful. "So that part is true. The two of them are at odds."

Fiona picked a stick of teriyaki out of the carton. "I guess so. At least Maynard didn't lie about that. But maybe they both have bad intentions."

"Good point." Morgan turned to Calvin. "Did you guys find anything in the old maps?"

"We think we might have gotten closer. If the lines we saw were the ley lines, then the epicenter is to the west of a little stream that runs through the woods," Cal said.

Fiona pointed at Cal with her chopstick. "I know that stream."

"Only problem is that some of the other landmarks seemed off, so we couldn't pinpoint it exactly," Cal said.

"Still, you got close. At least we know what direction to go," Luke said.

"And there's something else that might help." Celeste pushed her lo mein around with her chopsticks. "We found an old navigational instrument, and it's the same instrument that Rebekah's ghost keeps showing me. I think it might be something that could help us."

"Why?" Morgan asked, intrigued.

Celeste shrugged. "Rebekah kept gazing through it, and when I touched it, I felt a... resonance, I guess. It was cold and kind of... magnetic."

"Interesting," Morgan murmured, her mind whirring with the new information. "Fiona made a ring of stones to mute the effects of the center stone."

Fiona nodded. "And some protective necklaces to go with Morgan's sage-and-rosemary spray, so the two of those should help protect us from any weird creatures that are in the woods."

"Great." Jolene glanced out into the dark. "I know we only have three more days, but I don't think we want to venture out there in the dark. How about we get up early tomorrow and head in at first light?"

CHAPTER 18

Morgan awoke before dawn, a knot in her stomach. She dressed quickly and went downstairs, the smell of coffee drawing her into the kitchen. Johanna was already up, sipping tea, her worried eyes meeting Morgan's.

"I couldn't sleep," Johanna said.

Morgan nodded. "Me either."

They sat in silence as pale light crept across the floor. The old house creaked and settled around them.

Johanna reached across the table and squeezed Morgan's hand. "Be careful out there today. I wish I could join you, lend my strength..." She trailed off, and Morgan knew she was thinking of the years lost to captivity, her power drained away.

"We'll be okay, Mom. We've got this." Morgan

hoped she sounded more confident than she felt. So much still unknown, so much at stake.

"Good. Then I'll make breakfast. Don't want you to go off hungry." Johanna rose and started pulling ingredients out of the fridge.

The clink of plates echoed through the quiet kitchen as Morgan set the table. A flutter of white outside the window drew her gaze. She peered out at the herb garden, illuminated by dawn's rosy glow. Impossibly, the herbs had shot up nearly a foot since yesterday, growing tall and wild. Morgan's breath caught. The magic was strengthening.

In the tangle of greenery, Belladonna rolled happily, crushing a large ferny plant beneath her snowy fur. Morgan recognized it—agrimony. Great. Now the cat would smell like apricots all day.

A prickle on the back of Morgan's neck made her turn. She peered into the gloomy woods. Among the gnarled trunks, a pair of yellow eyes stared back at her. Morgan gasped and stumbled back. What creature lurked in there?

"What is it?" Johanna asked from the stove.

"Just some odd animals at the forest edge."

As Morgan set down glasses of orange juice, the others began to arrive. Mateo and Luke were clean-shaven and sharp looking. Jake was still rumpled from sleep, his blond hair sticking up. Calvin squinted slightly without his glasses.

Fiona entered and laid the crystal necklaces on the table. There were enough for all of them including the guys. "Let's do this," she said. Her jaw was set, eyes glinting.

Morgan loved her sister's grit.

"First, we eat." Jake pulled a chair out for Fiona, and they all started to dig in.

"Pass the butter," Luke said, never one to let a dangerous assignment ruin his appetite.

Morgan slid the butter dish over and forked a plain scrambled eggs onto her plate beside the toasted English muffin.

The tension in the room was palpable as they ate breakfast. Morgan passed around small glass bottles of her homemade herbal spray. "This should help protect us in the woods today."

Everyone spritzed themselves liberally. Luke's nose scrunched as the pungent odor hit him. "I smell like baked chicken now," he complained.

Celeste chuckled and held up the brass navigational instrument, its needles trembling. "I think this thing can help us navigate the ley lines toward the epicenter. And I've been practicing some new spells to try once we find it."

Morgan wiped her mouth with a napkin and set it on her empty plate. Around the table, the others were finishing up as well. Celeste drained her glass of orange juice, and Calvin stuffed the last of his English muffin into his mouth.

Johanna stood and began gathering up the dishes.

"Let me help you with that," Jake said, grabbing a few plates.

Morgan met Fiona's eyes across the table. Her sister gave a slight nod. This was it. Time to head into the woods and find the source of the disturbance before it was too late.

Morgan took a deep breath. "Well, I guess we better get going," she said, pushing back her chair.

The others murmured agreement and also stood. Morgan watched Celeste tuck the sextant into her bag. Luke checked his gun and slid it into his waistband. Morgan had no idea what good a gun would be against paranormal forces, but one never knew what might help.

Johanna set the dishes in the sink and turned to face them, twisting her hands in her apron.

Morgan went over and hugged her mom tight. "We'll be okay," she whispered.

Johanna nodded and smiled. "I know."

Morgan stepped back and faced the group. "Let's

roll." She stepped outside, squinting in the bright morning sunlight.

Belladonna bounded over through the lush herb garden, meowing loudly. Bits of leaf and stem clung to the cat's pure-white fur.

Morgan bent to scratch Belladonna behind her ears. The cat bumped her head against Morgan's hand then trotted off toward the looming tree line, looking back over her shoulder as if making sure they were following.

Belladonna waited at the edge of the woods, tail swishing impatiently. With a little chirp, she bounded into the trees. They scrambled to keep up as she led them along winding deer trails and over mossy logs. The woods felt charged, humming with power. Morgan sprayed more of her herbal mist as they walked. It left a tingling, cleansing sensation on her skin.

They passed strange mysterious animals—phantom deer that were practically invisible, glowing frogs, rabbits walking on their hind legs. Their presence unsettled Morgan, even though they seemed unbothered by the group's passing.

Celeste held the brass instrument up to her face as they walked. "I can see them! They look like lines of light in the woods. But there are so many of them."

"Do they point in a specific direction?" Morgan asked.

Celeste shook her head. "The lines are going haywire. I can't get a clear reading."

"According to the maps, the epicenter is near where the stream turns toward the east." Cal pointed. "That's this way."

They pressed on, the trees closing in around them. Dark shadows stretched between the gnarled trunks, and vines curled from the branches like skeletal fingers. The air felt heavy, charged with power that raised the fine hairs on Morgan's arms. She shivered despite the late-summer heat.

A shriek split the eerie quiet, making them jump. Morgan's heart hammered against her ribs. She grabbed for her crystal amulet with one hand, the other hovering near the herbal spray on her belt. Another cry echoed through the trees, inhuman and chilling.

A dark form burst from the undergrowth, rushing straight for them. Celeste yelped and stumbled back. Morgan's finger found the spray nozzle.

Before she could use it, lightning crackled from Jolene's palms, arcing out to strike the creature. It recoiled with an unearthly wail, dissolving into wisps of shadow.

"Thanks," Morgan breathed.

Jolene nodded, eyes vigilant for more threats.

They continued on slowly. The trees and boulders around them shimmered as if reality were destabilizing. Strange rifts opened in the earth, glowing with unnatural light. Morgan skirted one, careful not to look into its hypnotic depths.

Beneath their feet, the earth began to shift as if reality itself was tearing at the seams. Small fissures appeared, glimmering with an ethereal light. These were not mere holes; they were gateways, openings to another realm, growing larger with each passing second.

Suddenly, one such portal expanded to an alarming size. Belladonna, unfazed by the phenomenon, sauntered over it as if strolling across a patch of sunlit grass. Trusting the feline's instincts, Jolene mirrored her steps, pressing forward with a steady gaze.

However, no sooner had she set foot on the shimmering surface than it gave way beneath her. One moment, she was solidly grounded, and the next, she was falling, her scream swallowed by the gaping maw of the portal.

"Jolene!" Morgan rushed forward, heart in her throat. But it was too late. Jolene was gone, swallowed by the mystical portal. Morgan turned desperately to the others. "What do we do?"

"No!" Mateo's shout echoed through the woods as Jolene disappeared into the glowing portal. He shrugged off his jacket, preparing to dive in after her.

But Luke was faster, grabbing Mateo around the waist and pulling him back. "We don't know where that leads!" Luke yelled over the noise of the shifting earth and whirling energy. "We can't lose you too!"

Morgan felt like she was in a nightmare, watching helplessly as her little sister vanished. But there was no time for panic. They had to act.

"We need rope," she said, her voice shaky but determined. She met Luke's gaze, seeing her own fear reflected at her. "And something to anchor it."

Without waiting for a response, Morgan turned and sprinted back toward the house. Her heart pounded in her ears, drowning out the eerie sounds of the woods and the rush of adrenaline coursing through her veins.

As she ran, dodging the strange rifts in reality, she caught sight of peculiar creatures out of the corners of her eyes. A skunk looked down at her from a tree branch. A chipmunk grinned with comically gigantic cheeks. And an acorn as big as a football sat incongruously in the middle of the path.

Shaking off her bewilderment, Morgan reached the house and flung open the door. Johanna was pacing by the window, wringing her hands and casting anxious glances outside. The sight of Morgan's frantic entrance seemed to amplify her distress.

"What happened?" Johanna asked, rushing over to Morgan.

"Jolene fell into a portal," Morgan gasped out between breaths.

"What?" Johanna looked stricken. "How do we get her back?"

"We're working on it," Morgan replied quickly, already moving toward the closet where they kept camping gear.

She pulled out several coils of rope and a few heavy-duty carabiners. As she was about to head back outside, a calm meow stopped her in her tracks. Belladonna was lounging on the windowsill, bathing in a patch of sunlight. The white cat seemed completely unfazed by the chaos, even going so far as to curl up for a nap.

Shaking her head at the absurdity, Morgan hoisted the rope over her shoulder and dashed back outside. Luke and Mateo were waiting, their faces grim.

As they prepared to head back into the woods, a voice from behind them stopped them in their tracks.

"What in the world are you guys doing?"

They turned as one to see Jolene standing there. She was soaking wet but looked otherwise unharmed. But the really weird thing was that standing beside her was Maynard Dove.

CHAPTER 19

Morgan was the first to rush forward, her relief palpable. "Jolene, thank heavens! Are you all right?" she asked, glancing at Maynard, who was also soaked.

Shivering, Jolene clutched her arms around herself. "One second, I was falling, and the next—splash! I was in the ocean just off the north beach."

Fiona's brow furrowed with concern as she handed Jolene her hoodie. "But that's right below us. How did you get out?"

Jolene looked at Maynard. "Mr. Dove saved me."

Wheezing slightly, Maynard straightened his soggy jacket. "I was trying to control the ley lines from the beach when I saw her go in." His voice trailed off into a series of ragged coughs.

Celeste, gripping her amulet, looked back at their house. "Let's get inside. You both need to warm up."

A violent sneeze shook Maynard, signaling urgency to the situation. They shuffled toward the welcoming glow of the kitchen, where Johanna was already boiling water for tea.

Johanna dropped what she was doing and embraced Jolene, relief washing over her face. "Thank goodness you're all right," Johanna murmured, holding Jolene tight despite the fact that now she was getting wet too.

Fiona was already rushing to grab towels, passing them to Jolene and Maynard. "Here, dry off. We've got some spare clothes, too, if you need them."

Jolene gave a weak smile as she accepted the towel. "I'm okay. Just a bit shaken up. And very confused how I ended up in the ocean." She scrubbed at her dripping hair, glancing uncertainly at Maynard.

The old wizard was wheezing and coughing as he dried his beard with the towel. Luke guided him to a chair near the fireplace, where Calvin and Mateo were building a fire. "We need to get you warmed up, sir."

"Thank you for saving me," Jolene said to Maynard, her voice steady despite the ordeal she'd just been through.

Maynard nodded, his eyes focusing on the brass instrument in Calvin's hands. "That's a celestrolabe, isn't it?" he asked, his tone suggesting he knew exactly what it was.

Morgan watched closely, feeling a strange sense of unease at the way Maynard was staring at the device.

"Calvin had it in his basement, and it seems to be able to see these invisible ley lines," Celeste said.

He nodded again, his gaze not wavering from the celestrolabe. "It will see the lines, but it won't do you much good with Sofie messing things up," Maynard said, his voice carrying a weight of warning.

"What do you mean?" Morgan asked.

"We only have two more days, and I can't control the lines and battle her much longer," Maynard added, each word imbued with the gravity of the situation. "Without being able to control them, we can't get to the epicenter to mitigate the effects of the alignment."

Silence fell over the room as they all absorbed the implications of his revelation. The tension was palpable. Morgan felt the responsibility pressing down on her shoulders.

"We need to figure out how to stop her," Morgan declared, her voice firm in spite of the fear trying to worm its way into her heart.

Jolene nodded, her eyes finding Morgan's. "We have to work together to find a solution," she stated, her voice strong and determined.

"Yes, we do," Maynard concurred, gaze still fixed on the celestrolabe. "But we have to be careful. Sofie is powerful, and she won't hesitate to use that power against us if she thinks it will help her achieve her goals."

Morgan nodded, her mind racing with possibilities. "What do you suggest we do?" she asked Maynard, hoping he held insights on how they might overcome this looming threat.

The elderly wizard glanced at the celestrolabe on the table then back at Morgan. "There is another device called a lumiscope," he began, his voice a low rumble in the quiet room. "It's an ancient piece of equipment—a blend of a clock and a compass." He made a circular motion with his hand as if to illustrate his point.

Morgan could almost see it in her mind's eye: a large, circular instrument with hands like a clock and an arrow like a compass. She imagined its surface covered in strange symbols and runes that pulsed with magical energy. "What does it do?" she asked, her curiosity piqued.

"The lumiscope has the ability to sense and manipulate ley lines," Maynard explained. "It can balance their energies and harmonize their frequencies."

Celeste nodded enthusiastically. "That makes perfect sense. I could feel how erratic the lines were when we were in the woods earlier. It was like they couldn't hold still."

"Yes, precisely," Maynard confirmed with a sage nod. "With Sofie meddling and magnifying the effects of the alignment, the ley lines have become impossible to control. But the lumiscope can mitigate her interference."

He grimaced, breaking into another fit of wheezing coughs. The fire now blazing in the hearth seemed to revive him slightly.

"I used to have the lumiscope in my possession. Our father gave it to me. Unfortunately, I haven't seen the lumiscope since Alex stole it," Maynard continued ruefully.

"But if we can find it," Jolene said hopefully, "we can use it to stabilize the ley lines and get to the epicenter?"

"Exactly." Maynard coughed.

"Where do you think we can find it?" Fiona asked.

"Well," cut in Johanna, who had been silently

listening, "the celestrolabe and the crystals all ended up at Calvin's pawn shop. Maybe it's there."

"It could be, but I think I have a better idea," Luke said. "We can go straight to Alex. If he stole it, he probably knows where it is."

"Are you sure Sheriff White isn't here?" Fiona glanced around the police department parking lot to make sure one of the two town cruisers was gone.

"Relax, Fi," Jake reassured her, a lopsided grin on his face. "I called Tony. Sheriff White's out on a call, so we're in the clear."

The duo dashed across the parking lot and through the station's double doors, the overhead fluorescent lights illuminating the familiar sight of Deb sitting behind the glass at the front desk. Her eyes brightened at the sight of the pastry box Jake and Fiona had picked up on the way.

"Well, if it isn't my favorite baker," she quipped,

dusting powdered sugar off her uniform. "You sure know how to make a gal feel special, Jake. But I gotta ask, why the bribe? Cells are empty."

Jake's brows furrowed in confusion. "What do you mean? What about Alex Summers?"

Debra shook her head, swallowing the last bite of her donut. "Bailed out this morning."

Fiona's heart skipped a beat as she exchanged a worried glance with Jake. Who would bail out Alex?

"Do you know who bailed him out?" Jake asked, his voice barely above a whisper.

Deb scrolled through her computer, fingernails clacking on the keys, eyes squinting at the screen. Finally, she looked up. "It says here that someone named Sofie Dove bailed him out."

Jake and Fiona stood frozen, mirroring one another's disbelief. "Sofie Dove?" Fiona repeated, her voice a quiet echo in the empty police station.

Deb, still sitting behind her desk, looked between the two of them, an eyebrow arched. "Yeah," she responded, leaning back in her chair. "That's what it says here." She jabbed a finger at her computer screen, her mouth forming a thin line.

Jake and Fiona exchanged another glance, their minds whirling with questions. Alex Summers and Sofie Dove—how did they fit together? Jake had grilled Alex in the jail cell just days before, and not once had Alex mentioned any connection to Sofie Dove.

"Are you sure about this, Deb?" Jake asked again, his voice carrying a hint of desperation.

Deb rolled her eyes at him, her hands moving away from the keyboard to cross over her chest defensively. "I'm not blind yet, Jake Cooper," she retorted, the usual twinkle in her eyes replaced by a steely glare. "That's what it says right here."

With a final shared look of bewilderment, Jake and Fiona thanked Deb for the information and made their way back outside into the crisp afternoon air of Noquitt.

"Something's not right," Jake muttered as they walked down the sidewalk. His hand slipped into his pocket to pull out his phone. "I knew Alex was holding something back when I talked to him."

Fiona nodded in agreement. "Why would Alex keep quiet about knowing Sofie? And why would she bail him out?"

As they spoke, their eyes swept over their surroundings. Noquitt was as peaceful as ever with people milling about their day-to-day activities, completely oblivious to the brewing storm hidden within the nearby woods.

The strange occurrences that had been happening around them—the unusually fast-growing herbs in Morgan's garden, the portals, the strange animals in the woods—were confined to the Blackmoore property for now. But for how long?

"We need to let the others know," Jake said, breaking Fiona's train of thought. He was already dialing a number on his phone—most likely Morgan's.

Fiona sighed, looking back at the police station. The mundane building suddenly seemed a lot more sinister.

"Yeah," she agreed, her mind racing with possible scenarios and outcomes. "Now more than ever, we need to find Sofie Dove."

MORGAN ENDED the call with Jake and set her phone on the kitchen table with a contemplative look. Johanna, Jolene, Luke, Mateo, and Calvin were gathered around, having just heard the unsettling news about Sofie Dove's involvement with Alex Summers.

"I can't believe Sofie bailed Alex out of jail," Morgan said. "She acted like she didn't even know him when she came to the shop."

Johanna shook her head. "This changes things.

Maybe Maynard is the one we should be trusting. If Alex stole the lumiscope for Sofie, they must be working together."

"But that doesn't make sense," Jolene argued. "If they were working together, why would Alex pawn the stones instead of giving them directly to Sofie?"

Mateo nodded. "There's more going on here than we realize. I think we need to talk to Sofie directly and get some answers."

"And for that, we need to know where she lives." Jolene turned to the computer, her fingers flying over the keyboard as she dove through digital archives and databases. The glow of the screen illuminated her intense expression as she searched.

"Got it!" she declared. "I found Sofie's address."

"Maynard said that he didn't think Sofie would be out in the field somewhere, bending the ley lines to her will," Morgan said.

"Yes, but since we don't know where she would be, her house is a good start." Jolene picked up her phone. "I'll let Jake and Fiona know."

Jolene shot off a text, and her phone pinged immediately. "They're not far from the address. Jake said he'll check it out and let us know."

"So I guess we wait." Johanna reached into the

fridge and pulled out a Tupperware container. "Good thing I have cookies."

They moved into the sitting room, nibbling chocolate cookies and pacing as they waited for Jake's response.

The muted roars of the ocean, normally soothing, only added to the uneasy atmosphere. Belladonna wove between their legs, her purring a sharp contrast to the anxiety in the room. Morgan knelt to pet her, hoping for some measure of calm from her furry companion.

"I just hope Jake and Fiona are careful," Johanna said, staring out at the darkening sky through the big picture windows. "Sofie might not be very friendly."

Luke glanced at his watch. "They should be there by now. Let's hope they find something useful."

Out on the lawn, dandelions were springing up at an unnatural pace. The usually green expanse was quickly turning into a sea of yellow heads bobbing in the wind. It was a clear sign that magic was getting stronger in the area.

Suddenly, a zap of energy lit up the forest edge bordering their property. They all turned to look at it —an electrifying display that lasted only seconds but left an afterimage on their retinas.

Morgan's heart pounded in her chest. "We can't just sit here," she said. "We need that lumiscope."

Jolene nodded, subconsciously reaching for her protective amulet. "We need to find Sofie or Alex. And we need to do it fast."

But with no leads and no idea where to start, they could do nothing but wait for Jake and Fiona's report from Sofie's place and hope they would bring back answers and not more questions.

"Let's not waste time. If Jake doesn't find anything at Sophie's, what's our next plan?" Luke asked.

"We need to figure out where she is," Morgan said.

"Meow!" Belladonna leapt onto the back of the tallest chair in the room. Her ice-blue eyes were locked on something unseen in the distance, her tail flicking restlessly.

"Easier said than done." Jolene wiped cookie crumbs from her mouth.

"Yeah, but if anyone can figure it out, you can." Mateo smiled at Jolene.

"Patterns of behavior are important," Jolene added, her professional experience as a private investigator lending weight to her words. "If she consistently does the opposite of what Maynard expects, then that's a pattern we can work with."

Before anyone could respond to Jolene's comment,

Celeste entered the room, a thoughtful expression on her face.

"I talked to some dead ancestors, but I couldn't find anything concrete about ley lines or how to control them," Celeste admitted, a hint of frustration coloring her voice. "But Rebekah did mention something interesting about Maynard and Sofie."

The room fell silent as they waited for Celeste to continue.

"She said that those two have always been at odds," Celeste said slowly. "Maynard always tried to control things with brute force, while Sofie preferred a more natural approach. And no matter what Maynard suggested or believed in, Sofie would invariably do the exact opposite."

Morgan exchanged glances with Jolene. The pieces were starting to fall into place.

Belladonna made another agile leap, her body arcing high before landing gracefully on the top shelf of the bookcase. Miraculously, she didn't knock over any books. As Morgan watched her, a connection sparked in her mind.

She turned to look at her sisters, their faces filled with determination and worry. Celeste's revelation about the Dove siblings' dynamics was starting to make sense in a whole new way.

"If Maynard is drawn to the sea's level at the beach," she began slowly, voicing the thought that was forming in her mind, "then Sofie... she'd go high. The cliffs!"

Jolene, Fiona, and Celeste blinked at Morgan, their expressions blank as they digested her words. A ripple of understanding swept over them, and their faces lit up with recognition. Celeste nodded, her blond hair bobbing with the movement, while Fiona's fingers drummed thoughtfully on the table.

"Give me a sec," Jolene said, her voice full of determination. She pulled the laptop toward her, her fingers nimbly typing. "We have a couple of high clings, but I'll get the coordinates for the highest cliff peak in Noquitt."

As Jolene was engrossed with the computer, the shrill ring of Morgan's cell sliced through the air. Jake's name flashed on the screen, and she snatched it up, pressing it to her ear.

"Sofie's not at her place." Jake's voice echoed through the line, sounding frustrated.

"I think we've got a lead on where she might be," Morgan responded. She glanced over at Jolene, who nodded and rattled off some coordinates that Morgan relayed to Jake. "Meet you guys there in twenty minutes."

With their destination deduced and a plan form-ing, it was time to act. Mateo, Luke, and Calvin quickly gathered ropes and hiking gear from around the house—tools they might need depending on what they found at the cliffs.

CHAPTER 21

Morgan's pulse thudded in her ears as she led her sisters through the underbrush toward the jagged cliffs. The forest seemed to hum with a vibrancy that prickled against her skin, causing her intuition to flutter with warning. They moved like shadows, silent and swift, taking each step with deliberate care.

The normally tranquil woods felt charged, alive with an eerie undercurrent that seeped into their bones. An ominous breeze ruffled their hair and made the leaves dance wildly on their branches. Even the wildlife acted strangely, with birds circling in dizzying patterns above them and squirrels chattering in an unnerving discordant chorus.

Morgan held up a hand, signaling for them to stop.

The trees thinned here, giving way to a rocky outcrop that sloped steeply toward the cliff's edge. She peered through a thicket of hawthorn, squinting against the glaring sunlight that bounced off the ocean below. A lone figure stood at the edge of the precipice, a billowing green cape fluttering around her like an emerald cloud.

"She's here," Morgan whispered.

The sisters crouched low behind a large boulder, eyes trained on Sofie Dove.

Huddled behind the sheltering boulder, Morgan glanced at each of her companions. Luke's eyes were hard, a predator ready for the chase. Celeste, on the other hand, wore an expression of thoughtful caution. The sisters exchanged glances, a silent conversation flowing between them.

"Luke," Morgan began, her voice low but steady, "we don't want to escalate this more than necessary. We'll try talking first."

Luke's jaw clenched, but he nodded, his gaze never leaving Sofie Dove's solitary figure. Celeste let out a soft sigh of relief.

Taking a deep breath to steady her nerves, Morgan stepped from behind the boulder. Her boots crunched on the rocky terrain as she moved into the open.

"Sofie!" Her voice echoed across the cliffs, swallowed by the crashing waves below. The wind caught her hair and whipped it around her face as she stood there, exposed and vulnerable.

Sofie turned with unhurried grace, her eyes wide with surprise that quickly melted into cool composure. "Morgan," she acknowledged, her gaze flickering to take in the group emerging from their hiding spot. "I see you've brought reinforcements."

Morgan forced a tight smile onto her face. "We're concerned, Sofie."

Sofie's eyebrows lifted slightly as she folded her arms across her chest. "Oh?"

"It's about Alex Summers," Fiona chimed in, stepping up next to Morgan. Her red curls gleamed brightly under the sun, a stark contrast to the tension that lined her face.

"Alex?" Sofie's gaze flicked toward Fiona before returning to Morgan. "What about him?"

"You never mentioned you knew him, yet you bailed him out of jail," Jolene stated bluntly from behind them. Her sky-blue eyes bored into Sofie with unwavering intensity.

Sofie didn't flinch at the accusation but instead tilted her head slightly. "And why would that concern you?" Her voice held a note of challenge.

"It concerns us because you lied, Sofie," Morgan

said, meeting the older woman's gaze squarely. "The alignment is coming, and you're disrupting our ability to reach the epicenter. We need to stop the worst from happening."

Sofie's laughter died down as she regarded Morgan with a look that bordered on pity. "Oh, you poor, misguided girls." She sighed dramatically. "You're looking in the wrong direction. It's my brother who's causing the disruption."

Jolene stepped forward then, her blue eyes flashing with anger. "Stop lying, Sofie!" she snapped. "We're onto you, and so is Maynard. He's trying to help. He even saved me."

Something flickered in Sofie's eyes at Jolene's words—a momentary softening that was quickly replaced by steely resolve.

"Is that so?" she retorted coolly. "Well, if Maynard is such a good guy, maybe he should consider giving up some of his power to save everyone from the effects of the alignment. He hasn't done that, has he? No, I didn't think so, because I'm the one that is trying to help, and he is the one making things difficult."

The sisters glanced at each other at Sofie's words. There was an edge to her voice that hadn't been there before—a hint of desperation beneath her usual confident facade. Morgan felt a twinge of unease but pushed it aside.

"If that's the case, then, why did you lie about knowing Alex?" Fiona asked.

"And why did you have him pawn the stones? You did, didn't you?" Jolene added.

"And why did you have him steal the lumiscope?" Celeste chimed in.

Sofie raised her brows at Celeste's question. She sighed and turned to them. "Yes, I had Alex working for me. But I did it for the good of everyone," Sofie admitted, her voice a mere whisper against the ocean's roar.

Morgan glanced at her sisters, their faces mirroring her own surprise. The green-cloaked woman had been orchestrating things from the shadows all along.

"He stole the stones and pawned them because I knew Calvin would sell them to you," Sofie continued, her gaze never leaving Morgan's. "I wanted you Black-moores to have them in your possession so they wouldn't reach the epicenter."

A scoff escaped Morgan's lips before she could stop it. "Why all the intrigue, Sofie? Why not just give them to us directly?"

Sofie sighed, a gust of wind catching her cloak and

sending it billowing around her. "It's simple," she replied. "I didn't want Maynard to find out you had them. If he did, he would insinuate himself into your plans, and things wouldn't turn out well."

Morgan felt a knot of frustration tighten in her stomach. They'd been used, manipulated into this game of magical keep-away with an impending celestial disaster hanging over their heads.

"But alas," Sofie said with a bitter laugh that was carried away by the wind, "it looks like all my efforts were for nothing. You didn't keep the stones, and Maynard has insinuated himself into your plans anyway."

"If what you say is true, you won't mind helping us out," Celeste said.

Sofie's lips curled into a smirk. "How, exactly, do you propose I help you?" she asked, her voice dripping with sarcasm. "You've already lost the stones."

Celeste stepped forward, her expression determined. "We need the lumiscope to keep the lines from flickering so we can find the epicenter."

Sofie's brows furrowed in a scowl. "What makes you think you need it?"

Celeste cast a quick glance at Morgan before replying, "We have the celestrolabe, but the ley lines are jittery. Maynard said the lumiscope will help keep them straight. We need it to find the epicenter."

A laugh burst from Sofie's lips then, high and clear against the crash of the waves below. "I do have the lumiscope, but perhaps you should think twice before putting your trust in Maynard."

"Or in you," Morgan said. "If you really were the one that wanted to help us, you'd hand it over."

With a sigh of resignation, Sofie reached into her cloak and pulled out an intricate device that gleamed in the afternoon sunlight. The lumiscope.

The device was roughly the size of a small compact, shiny gold decorated with gemstones and complex etchings.

Sofie held it out to them, her expression unreadable. Morgan stepped forward to take it, her fingers brushing against Sofie's as she did so. A jolt of energy passed between them, causing Morgan to flinch slightly.

Sofie retracted her hand and tucked it back into her cloak, her gaze following the lumiscope as Morgan handed it over to Celeste.

They had what they had come for, but instead of relief, a knot of dread settled in Morgan's stomach.

"Thank you," Celeste said, her voice sounding small in the vast expanse of the cliffside.

Sofie merely nodded, her gaze lingering on the lumiscope a moment longer before she turned away from them. "Remember what I said about Maynard," she warned over her shoulder as she focused her attention on the invisible ley lines.

As they turned to leave, Morgan couldn't shake off the nagging feeling that they had just made a monumental mistake.

CHAPTER 22

The Blackmoore kitchen buzzed with electricity as they prepared for another trip into the forest.

Fiona paced before the granite countertops, her curls bouncing with each step. She held up a burlap bag. "I have the stones that will mute the powers of the yellow crystals. Celeste has the lumiscope that will hopefully lead us to the epicenter." She paused and turned to the rest of them. "But what about those portals? We can't just wander into the woods blind."

Jolene stood by the window, her gaze piercing through to the woods beyond. "Last time I fell into one of those things, I ended up taking an unplanned swim. I'm not eager to find out where I'd land next."

Calvin leaned against the island, his glasses

reflecting the overhead lights as he studied an array of maps spread out before him. "We could try to predict their locations," he suggested. "Map out safe paths based on where they appeared last."

Celeste nibbled on her lip, a habit when she was deep in thought. "And if new ones open up? We can't possibly map them all. The clock is ticking, and we need to get back in there before nightfall. We need a way to protect ourselves from the portals."

"Astrid said we'd need spells, sticks, and stones. Maybe a spell?" Mateo suggested.

"Meow!" Belladonna stood in front of the door, her gaze wavering between it and the humans.

Morgan let her out, and the cat bounded over to the herb garden. The plants had grown a good foot since the morning. Belladonna went straight for the overgrown agrimony, rolling ecstatically among the fragrant leaves and yellow blooms and looking back at Morgan every few seconds.

"She seems very interested in that herb," Fiona murmured, moving closer to the window. "She was rolling in it the other day too."

Belladonna looked back at Morgan, and their eyes locked. A realization sparked in Morgan's mind. "It must be the agrimony!"

"Huh?" Jolene joined them at the window.

"Belladonna could walk right over the portals. I think the agrimony she'd rolled in right before protected her."

Jolene's eyes widened. "Guess we'd better go join her."

Morgan burst through the back door, her sisters and the guys close behind. The pungent aroma of the overgrown agrimony washed over them as they raced into the garden.

"Hurry, grab as much as you can!" Morgan called out, already yanking up handfuls of the yellow-flowered herb and stuffing the leaves and blooms into her pockets.

The others fanned out, following her lead. Fiona tore off sprigs with quick, deft movements while Jolene simply scooped up entire plants, roots dangling. Calvin and Celeste gathered carefully, trying not to damage the growth.

Within minutes, they were all laden with the fragrant bundles. Morgan brushed her hands off on her jeans, smiling. "Looks like we've got plenty now. It's lucky the garden has been growing like crazy."

Jolene inhaled deeply from a bunch she held. "Yeah, perfect timing. But how much do we actually need for protection?"

"Good question." Morgan glanced at Belladonna,

who sat nearby, grooming her agrimony-dusted fur. "She just rolled around in it. I'm guessing if we rub some on exposed skin and fill our pockets, it should work the same for us."

"Let's hope so," Calvin said, eyeing the dark woods. "Otherwise, this expedition is going to get dicey fast."

The group followed Morgan's example, crushing leaves and flowers between their hands before smoothing the juices and oils over any bare skin.

Once their pockets bulged with bundles and they were sufficiently coated, Morgan did a final check. "All right, I think we're ready."

Morgan looked around at everyone. They all nodded, their expressions a mix of determination and apprehension.

"Okay, let's do this," she said, her voice sounding steady despite the knot of nerves in her stomach.

They gathered up the rope, lumiscope, and celestrolabe. The woods seemed darker and creepier than ever, the trees looming and casting dark shadows. Belladonna trotted ahead, her white fur glowing faintly in the shadows.

The air was thick with tension, the silence broken only by the occasional rustle of leaves, the distant hoot of an owl, and the scurrying sounds of something just out of their line of vision.

Suddenly, a giant portal opened in front of them, a swirling vortex of darkness that seemed to suck in the very light around it. Belladonna barely hesitated before trotting right over it. She stopped on the other side and looked back at them.

Morgan's heart pounded. She knew they had to follow, but the thought of stepping into that portal filled her with dread.

Jolene took a step forward. "I'll go first," she said.

Morgan grabbed her arm, pulling her back. "No, I'll go first."

Jolene protested, but Morgan shook her head. "I'm the oldest. It's my responsibility."

Taking a deep breath, she stepped onto the edge of the portal. The swirling darkness seemed to reach up for her, but she resisted its pull. She closed her eyes and took a step forward.

Nothing happened.

She opened her eyes, surprised to find herself still there, standing on top of the portal as if it didn't even exist. Belladonna watched from other side, her tail swishing impatiently.

"I guess the agrimony works," she said and went to join the cat.

One by one, they stepped across the portal. Everyone made it through safely.

Belladonna trotted ahead again, leading them through the woods. They followed her, their eyes darting from side to side, half expecting something to jump out at them from the shadows.

Celeste worked the celestrolabe and lumiscope, following the faint glimmering trails of the ley lines through the dark woods. The instruments led them deeper into the forest, past gnarled oaks and shadowy undergrowth.

Nature's rules seemed inverted here. A raccoon with luminous feathers instead of fur waddled curiously toward them, its gaze glowing green in the dark. Nearby, a chorus of frogs croaked in what sounded eerily like harmony, all while a crow with a long, peacock-like tail flew overhead, cawing melodically. The trees themselves seemed to shift and elongate as the group walked by, stretching impossibly high.

The hair on Morgan's neck prickled as the shadows around them swayed and rippled, though there was no wind. She gripped her amulet tightly, the obsidian smooth and reassuring against her palm.

Celeste peered through the celestrolabe as she held the lumiscope before her, brows drawn in concentration as she worked to focus on the ley lines. But Morgan could see beads of sweat on her sister's forehead. The effort of trying to keep the lines straight while navigating the forest was taking its toll.

Energy snapped all around them, and the air grew thick. Walking became more difficult, like trudging through waist-high water.

"It's too much," Celeste said through gritted teeth. "It's like the magic is fighting us."

As if in response, a tree branch directly above them splintered with a deafening crack. Cal pulled Celeste back just before it crashed down where she had stood.

The energetic hum in the air increased. Morgan raised her arm against the powerful wind, squinting to see through the leaves and debris whipping past.

"I can sense that we are close. If we can just push through and make it beyond that clump of twisted oak trees up ahead!" She glanced back at Celeste, who was clutching the lumiscope in a white-knuckled grip. Celeste gave a subtle nod, confirming they were nearing their destination.

The wind swelled, pushing them back with an almost physical force. Morgan's hair lashed at her face like whips. She gritted her teeth and bowed her head as she forced one foot in front of the other.

"This must be the time we need a spell!" Jolene yelled.

Celeste began reciting a spell, her voice rising to carry over the roar of the wind. Morgan felt a surge of magical energy release from her sister. But instead of propelling them forward, it ricocheted back, slamming them against the trees behind them.

Morgan grunted as her back hit rough bark. They were pinned there, unable to take another step forward against the wind and misdirected magic.

"It's the wrong incantation!" Celeste yelled over the gale. "My magic is just bouncing back at us!"

Morgan craned her neck to peer through the trees. She could just make out a pulsing aura—the epicenter. It had to be. They were so close!

If they could only get past these blasted trees...

Morgan shifted against the tree, trying to wiggle free, but the force was too strong. They were stuck. She looked back at the others plastered against their own trees. Fiona's curls thrashed wildly across her face. Jolene had her eyes squeezed shut.

They had to retreat, regroup, and try again. Morgan turned her head toward Celeste and yelled, "We have to fall back! It's too much!"

Celeste gave a frustrated nod and stopped chanting. The wind seemed to let up ever so slightly without her spell pushing against it.

Together, they managed to stumble away from the

trees and back down the path. The wind died down with each step until they were able to stop and catch their breath.

Morgan glanced back once more at the area they'd nearly breached. So close...

"What was that all about?" Jolene asked.

"Something doesn't want us to get to the epicenter," Mateo said.

Fiona clutched the burlap bag and looked back behind them. "Should we try again?"

It was getting dark in the woods. Morgan looked at her watch. It would soon be night. Facing whatever lay ahead in this forest at night was not a risk they could take. "I think we need to retreat and regroup. I don't know about you guys, but I'm tired and weak. We'll need all our strength when we reach the epicenter."

The others nodded, weariness and frustration evident on their faces.

The journey home remained fraught with odd occurrences and supernatural obstacles, but the agrimony allowed them to bypass the mystifying portals. They finally emerged from the tree line, the Blackmoore house a welcome sight.

Inside, they collapsed in the sitting room, the day's exhaustion settling heavily on their shoulders.

Belladonna trotted around to each person, sniffing them as if to ensure they were okay.

"We were so close this time," Fiona said, dropping her head into her hands.

"We're going to have to figure out how to get past all of that," Jake said. "Maybe more herbs or stones?"

"We already have those two parts, so it's the spell, I think." Celeste shrugged. "Sorry, guys. I thought I had that nailed."

"It's not your fault," Morgan rushed to console her. "Besides, that might not even be where we need the spell."

Celeste frowned. "What do you mean?"

"I'm not sure. I think all the chaos in there stems from Maynard and Sofie fighting against each other with the ley lines."

"Good point," Luke said. "We need to broaden our thinking."

Johanna bustled into the sitting room bearing a tray laden with still-warm chocolate chip cookies and steaming mugs of hot cocoa topped with mini marsh-mallows.

"You all look exhausted," she tutted, setting the tray on the table. "What happened out there?"

They brought Johanna up to speed as they sipped the cocoa.

"I'm glad you're all okay," Johanna said. "Sounds like you need to figure out what to do to get further into the woods."

Celeste shook her head slowly. "I still think a spell can help. But I tried a transportation spell earlier, and the wind practically ripped it out of my hands. It felt like a warning."

Luke leaned forward to grab another cookie. "Maybe we're overthinking this now. We're exhausted. I say we all get some rest and revisit it tomorrow with fresh eyes. Sometimes, the subconscious works things out while we sleep."

Morgan nodded, the wisdom in Luke's words settling over her. The day's events had drained them, both physically and mentally. Even now, her thoughts felt sluggish, as if wading through molasses.

Glancing around, she saw the same bone-weary exhaustion mirrored on the others' faces. Fiona slumped on the sofa, eyes half-closed as she picked at a loose thread on a throw pillow. Mateo stared blankly into the fire, chin propped in his hand. Only Belladonna seemed unfazed as she napped peacefully in her plush cat bed.

Calvin set his empty mug on the coffee table. "Luke's right. We need sleep more than anything now.

My brain feels fried after everything we just went through."

"Mine too," Celeste murmured through a yawn. "I can barely keep my eyes open."

Johanna started to gather up the mugs and plates. "You should all get some rest. Things will look clearer in the morning."

Morgan met her mother's eyes, reading the concern there. Johanna was worried for them but knew better than to discourage their efforts. All Johanna could do was to have faith in them and provide grounding when they needed it most.

Morgan tried to offer a reassuring smile. "We'll figure it out. Don't worry. A good night's sleep is probably the best thing for us right now."

Her mother smiled softly in return before disappearing down the hall toward the kitchen. The others began shuffling tiredly toward their rooms.

Morgan stood, joints creaking in protest. She stretched her arms over her head. "All right. Let's pick this up again in the morning. I think we could all use a good night's sleep."

The others murmured agreement, slowly getting to their feet.

They filed sleepily out of the sitting room toward their bedrooms, each lost in thought. Morgan paused in the hallway, watching Celeste continue on, still frowning slightly in concentration. She clearly wasn't ready to let the spell question go yet.

With a sigh, Morgan entered her own bedroom. She peeled off her jeans and sweatshirt and dropped them on the floor before collapsing into bed. The soft mattress enveloped her tired body. She was asleep almost instantly.

CHAPTER 23

The shrieking beeps of the smoke detector jerked Morgan from sleep. She scrambled out from under her blankets and bolted down the stairs into the kitchen. Wisps of smoke led her to their coffee maker, but it was the eruption of green stems and coffee-plant leaves spilling out that halted her on the threshold.

"What in the world?" Fiona's voice echoed Morgan's shock from just behind her.

Morgan could only shake her head and shrug. The magical disorder they'd grappled with was clearly escalating.

Shutting down the smoking appliance, the sisters migrated outside to inspect the garden. The herbs had taken on a life of their own. Peppermint and spearmint towers loomed over them, and fennel fronds performed an airy dance in the slight breeze.

Morgan furrowed her brow. "Never seen herbs skyrocket like this, even with a touch of magic."

Fiona's frown mirrored her concern. "The alignment's really ramping up," she said.

Something caught Morgan's eye near the fence—a fluttering figure she mistook for a seagull. But as it launched into the air, they made out a tail that streamed far beyond its body. Even Belladonna seemed disturbed as she watched the bird fly awkwardly over the ocean.

"It's starting to affect things outside of the forest. We have no time to waste." Morgan turned back toward the kitchen.

Luke, Jake, and Cal had shown up.

Mateo came in from the front hall and stopped short. "What's up with the coffee machine?"

"The alignment," Morgan said.

Mateo raised his brows. "Jolene isn't going to be happy about that."

Johanna burst into the room, apron strings flying. "I'll get a pot going in the other machine. Who's up for pancakes?"

Despite the burgeoning supernatural storm, Johanna's normality was a comforting constant, and they all needed to eat before tackling the forest again.

Jake and Mateo set the table as the room filled with the scent and sounds of sizzling bacon and frying eggs.

Jolene strode into the kitchen, eyeing the bizarre plant sprouting from the K-Cup machine. "Please tell me there's still coffee."

Johanna gestured warmly to the pot she'd brewed in their old coffee maker. "Fresh batch just finished. Have a seat, and I'll bring you some pancakes."

Jolene sank into a chair with relief, accepting the mug Mateo passed her way.

Luke set down his fork, glancing around the table. "Did anyone come up with any brilliant ideas overnight for how to handle the alignment?"

Head shakes and murmured "no's" answered him.

"It feels right that we need a spell," Morgan said, "but for what exactly?"

"The stones, the ley lines, the epicenter... there's a few options," Fiona replied.

Jake nodded slowly. "We need to get it right, though. We don't have time for second-guessing."

Morgan set down her mug. "You're right. We need to think through this logically."

Jolene tapped her fingers on the side of her mug.

"Our goal is to get to the epicenter and stop the stones from aligning, right?"

Everyone around the table nodded.

"Okay, so we've got the sticks covered already," Jolene continued. "The herbs let us walk over the portals, no problem."

Fiona chimed in. "And I have my stones that will help neutralize the alignment crystals' powers."

"Exactly—the stones are handled too," Morgan said. "So it makes sense the spell must be for whatever is preventing us from reaching the epicenter itself."

"Yes, but what, exactly, is preventing us from reaching it?" Mateo asked.

Jolene straightened, speaking up. "Maybe Celeste had some insight overnight."

Calvin looked up from his pancakes, brow furrowing. "Hey, where is Celeste anyway?"

CELESTE SAT cross-legged on the rug in the mansion's library, eyes closed in meditation. She took slow, deep breaths, focusing her energy and intention on connecting with Rebekah. Rebekah hadn't really given her any useful information thus far, but no other spirits seemed to want to talk to her. Perhaps she had just been asking the wrong questions.

As Celeste centered her awareness, she sensed Rebekah's presence nearby. Opening her eyes, Celeste was not surprised to see the ghostly figure of a woman in a pale-blue dress hovering near the shelves of leather-bound books.

"Rebekah, I need your help," Celeste said. "What do you know of the celestial alignment that is coming and the Dove family? Have you heard stories from your elders about it?"

The spirit tilted her head thoughtfully before responding. "As I've told you before, I do not possess firsthand accounts, my dear. However, whispers from my grandmother's era do mention the Dove siblings in a good light."

Celeste was surprised to hear Rebekah speak well of the Dove siblings. She leaned forward eagerly. "How were Sofie and Maynard seen in a good light back then?" she asked.

Rebekah floated languidly around the library, ghostly fingers trailing over the leather-bound spines. "From what I recall of the whispered stories, they joined forces to wield some ancient magic that stopped powerful dark forces from wreaking havoc."

The spirit paused by the window, gazing out at the

herb garden. "Of course, the details escape me." She turned back to the books, leaning close and taking a big whiff, then closed her eyes blissfully. "Ahh, the scent of leather-bound books always stirs my heart."

Celeste pressed for more information. "Were Sofie and Maynard around during your time? You said the stories were from your grandmother's era."

"Yes, they existed then but were quite young," Rebekah replied. "As you know, those two are ancient and powerful sorcerers. In my time, they were not close siblings. More like feuding rivals."

"Feuding?" Celeste asked. "What was their feud about?"

Rebekah shrugged, her filmy blue sleeves billowing. "Ah, the complexities of family. Siblings often quarrel, do they not?"

Celeste thought for a moment. She didn't remember much conflict with her own sisters. But perhaps understanding the ancient feud between Sofie and Maynard held the key to unlocking the current mysteries around the celestial alignment.

"Well, my sisters and I usually get along," Celeste admitted, watching Rebekah drift around the library. "We have our disagreements, of course, but nothing like a centuries-old feud."

Rebekah paused in her ghostly meandering to face

Celeste. "Well, my dear, it's not so for everyone. Perhaps that difference holds some clue to your dilemma."

Celeste furrowed her brows. "You mean the way we work together as sisters might be key to solving this?"

Rebekah merely smiled, her translucent form flickering like candlelight. "Perhaps," she said cryptically before moving on to inspect another row of books.

Celeste sighed in frustration. She appreciated Rebekah's guidance but wished the ghost could be more direct. With the celestial alignment approaching and its effects growing stronger by the day, they didn't have time for riddles.

Celeste watched as Rebekah's ghostly form slowly faded away, leaving her alone in the library once more.

She stood, stretching out her legs that had started to tingle after sitting cross-legged for so long. The smells of sizzling bacon and brewing coffee wafting in from the kitchen made Celeste's stomach rumble.

Celeste made her way toward the kitchen, where she could hear the clinking of plates and hum of conversation. Her sisters, along with Luke, Jake, Mateo, Calvin, and her mother, were gathered around the large table.

"There you are!" Fiona said, looking up from her

plate of pancakes. "We were just wondering where you were."

Celeste gave her a wry smile. "I was chatting with Rebekah, trying to get some insight about the Doves and the alignment."

"Learn anything useful?" Morgan asked, handing Celeste a mug of coffee.

"Maybe," Celeste replied vaguely, taking a long sip of the hot, fragrant drink. The caffeine helped further pull her mind back into focus.

As the group settled in around the table, passing platters of food, Celeste recounted her conversation with Rebekah. She shared the spirit's recollection of whispers about Sofie and Maynard joining forces long ago.

"Joining forces?" Mateo said incredulously, through a mouthful of bacon. "Hard to imagine those two working together after everything we've seen and heard."

Celeste nodded. "I know. But Rebekah seemed certain the story came from a reliable source."

"Perhaps they were different people back then," Morgan suggested thoughtfully.

"Or it's more fiction than fact, tales twisted over centuries of retelling," Fiona added skeptically.

Celeste sighed. "I wish Rebekah could have given

more concrete details. She hinted that the way we sisters work together might hold some key to solving this whole alignment situation."

"How do you mean?" asked Johanna as she refilled coffee mugs around the table.

"Well, we generally get along and collaborate despite our differences," Celeste explained. "Rebekah made it sound like Sofie and Maynard's relationship has been marred by feuding and rivalry for ages."

Johanna snorted. "I wouldn't say you girls always got along."

Morgan frowned. "Of course we did."

"Maybe you do now, but when you were little, I had to do a lot of refereeing," Johanna said.

Celeste listened thoughtfully as her mother described how she used to help her daughters reconcile after arguments when they were young.

"I guess you're right. We didn't always get along perfectly," Morgan admitted, leaning back in her chair. "I remember a few blow-up fights between Fiona and me as teens."

Fiona laughed. "Oh yeah, like when I deleted your save file on that video game you were obsessed with."

Morgan shot her sister a mock glare. "I was so mad! But Mom made us bake cookies together, and we ended up laughing about it afterward."

Johanna smiled at the memory. "Sometimes, all it takes is a reminder of how much you care for one another. Finding common ground can mend the deepest rifts between siblings."

"Easier said than done with Sofie and Maynard," Jake said dubiously, shaking his head. "We can barely get them in the same side of town, let alone baking cookies together."

"Jake's right. Those two have avoided each other for centuries, it seems," Jolene added. She absent-mindedly stroked Belladonna, who was curled up in her lap. "I'm not sure how we'd convince them to meet or what we could do to get them to reconcile."

Celeste thought for a moment, gazing out the window at the woods beyond. She recalled Rebekah's conviction that she and her sisters held the key.

"Maybe this is where the spell comes in," Celeste finally said.

Fiona leaned forward, brow furrowed. "What exactly would this spell do?"

Celeste took a sip of coffee, gathering her thoughts. She set down her mug and explained.

"Well, since Sofie and Maynard are both interested in the ley lines and claim they actually both want the same thing—to stop the alignment from causing harm —I think I could try a gathering spell."

She paused, seeing that she had everyone's attention.

"The spell would draw Sofie and Maynard closer to the epicenter," Celeste continued. "It would bring them to the same physical space, in close proximity."

Morgan's eyes widened. "You mean right here in our backyard?"

Celeste nodded. "Exactly."

"Okay, so let's say we get them here with this spell," Luke said slowly. "Then what? How do we actually get them to see they should work together?"

Celeste sighed. "That part, we'd have to figure out. But first, we need to get them in the same place."

As if on cue to emphasize the urgency, the old grandfather clock in the library chimed loudly. Celeste counted ten slow gongs marking the late-morning hour. Time was slipping away.

"We have to try something. We're running out of time," Morgan said decisively, standing up from the table. "If your spell can draw Sofie and Maynard here, then let's do it. We can work out the rest, but we need to act fast."

Celeste felt a swell of gratitude and relief at her sister's confidence in her. The others around the table also voiced their support.

But then she sighed, deflating the brief surge of hope her spell idea had inspired.

"There's just one problem," she said regretfully. "In order for a summoning spell to work, I would need to have something that belongs to each person I'm trying to draw in."

They sat in disappointed silence for a few moments, the only sounds the ticking clock and Belladonna's purring. Celeste racked her brain, trying to think of any possible solution.

Suddenly, Morgan perked up. "The lumiscope!" she exclaimed. "That's something of Sofie's we already have."

"You're absolutely right," Celeste said, feeling a spark of hope reignite. "The lumiscope can draw in Sofie."

"But we still have nothing from Maynard," Luke pointed out grimly.

Before the gloom could settle back in, Fiona jumped up from her seat. "I know!" she cried. "Hang on!"

She rushed from the room before anyone could respond. They heard her running up the stairs, and moments later, Fiona came running back in, clutching a small pouch.

"I can't believe I didn't think of this sooner," she

said breathlessly, holding up the bag. "The two stones, the nonmagical ones, are still here. I had a feeling I should keep them, and I guess this is why."

Celeste's eyes lit up. "Of course! Those originally came from Maynard, so they'll work."

"When can you do the spell?" Morgan asked.

Celeste considered for a moment. "Give me a few hours to gather some other ingredients from around the property and prepare." She stood, filled with a sense of purpose. "I'll need to find a space outdoors where the energy flows strongly. If you all can scout around, that would help."

As everyone dispersed throughout the house and yard, Celeste cradled the stones and lumiscope gently. She sent up a silent prayer that these objects would be enough to bring Sofie and Maynard together.

eleste sat cross-legged on the dewy grass, brow furrowed in concentration as she studied the ancient spell book laid out before her. The faintest hint of lavender wafted on the breeze, mingling with the earthier scents of sage and rosemary. Celeste inhaled deeply, letting the aromatic blend soothe her nerves.

Around her, the others formed a loose circle, radiating calm support. Jake and Calvin murmured quietly as they double-checked the carefully assembled ring of rocks, herbs, and crystals encircling Sofie's lumiscope and Maynard's stones.

Morgan knelt nearby, deftly weaving stems of rue and agrimony into fragrant smudge sticks. The herbs rustled, their leaves saturated with celestial energy.

At the edge of the garden, Luke kept watch, vigilant and ready to spring into action at the first sign of trouble. Though his stance was relaxed, tension thrummed through his muscular frame.

Morgan squeezed Celeste's shoulder reassuringly before moving to help Mateo and Jolene prepare a batch of strengthening elixir. The pungent, earthy aroma of burdock and dandelion wafted from their makeshift workstation.

Johanna stood serenely apart from the activity, her face creased with worry as the sun climbed higher in the sky.

Celeste took a steadying breath and resumed her study of the ancient text, murmuring the lyrical words under her breath. She had to get this right. The fate of Noquitt rested on drawing Sofie and Maynard together.

As she rehearsed the invocation, a flash of white at the corner of her eye drew her attention. Belladonna prowled the garden's edge, back arched and fur bristling. The cat's movements radiated anxiety as she paused to sniff the herb-heavy air. Her eyes narrowed to vivid blue slits.

With a delicate hop, Belladonna leapt lightly onto the weathered table beside Celeste, tail twitching as she eyed the open spell book. Tentatively, she reached out a white paw to pat the aged parchment, as if tapping out a feline beat of encouragement.

Celeste smiled softly at the cat's gesture, heart swelling with love for her intuitive companion.

Celeste took a deep, centering breath, steadying her nerves as she prepared to begin the incantation. She could feel the eyes of her friends and family upon her, their gazes filled with a mixture of hope and apprehension.

Closing her eyes, Celeste let the words flow, ancient syllables rolling lyrically off her tongue. Her voice was hushed yet strong, infused with power. The flames of the candles seemed to dance and sway in response as if moved by an unseen wind.

As Celeste continued the chant, she sensed a shift in the energies around her. The herbs and crystals of the circle hummed, resonating with her invocation. Even the plants of the garden stirred, leaves and stems bending subtly toward the heart of the ring in which she sat.

Her companions watched in awed silence, hardly daring to breathe for fear of disrupting the delicate magic at work. Jake and Cal exchanged an incredulous look, while Mateo's eyes were narrowed in concentration as he sought to analyze the forces being called forth.

Johanna observed calmly, though her hands were clasped before her in wordless hope and encouragement. Luke remained alert, prepared to act if any threat arose.

The power continued to build as Celeste wove her spell, binding the mystical elements together in anticipation of drawing forth Sofie and Maynard. She could feel the energy thrumming through her veins, at once exhilarating and terrifying in its sheer intensity.

Belladonna paced the perimeter, her white fur standing on end from the static charge in the air. Yet even the watchful feline seemed content to let the magic run its course.

Celeste realized she was nearing the invocation's crux, at which point she would call the feuding siblings by name, beseeching their presences. Her pulse quickened, and she took a final centering breath, drawing on the strength of her family and friends surrounding her.

As the final syllables left her lips, a sudden wind gusted through the garden, swirling leaves and petals into the air. The candle flames surged wildly before extinguishing in wisps of smoke.

Everyone was silent as the intense energy summoned by the spell dissipated.

Finally, Jolene spoke up. "Is that it? Did it work? When will we see them?"

Celeste shrugged. "I think it worked, but I'm not sure when we will see them."

"So what do we do now?" Jake asked.

Celeste turned to him. "Now, we wait."

CHAPTER 25

Morgan Blackmoore sat on the edge of the oversized chair, her fingers tapping a restless rhythm on the armrest. The clock in the corner chimed twice, marking two hours since they had started their vigil in the sitting room. Her sky-blue eyes were glued to the expansive picture window that overlooked their wild herb garden and the ominous woods beyond.

Her heightened intuition thrummed with anticipation, a low hum of energy beneath her skin. Every shadow that danced in the moonlight sent her heart racing, and every rustle of leaves had her hoping it was either Maynard or Sofie. Yet neither of them had shown up. The anticipation was suffocating.

The silence was finally shattered by Luke's worried

voice. "What if Maynard and Sofie decide not to pass by here? What if they take another route to the epicenter?"

His concern resonated in the room, causing a ripple of anxiety. It was a valid question. Their plan hinged on the two wizards passing through their yard as they made their way to the epicenter of the ley lines.

However, Celeste responded with an unwavering confidence that belied the tension in the room. "They will pass through here," she said, her blond curls bouncing as she nodded for emphasis. "The spell I cast ensures it. Our paths are intertwined for tonight."

Morgan looked at her sister and couldn't help but admire her determination. Celeste had come a long way from being a novice spell caster, and now, they were depending on her.

Morgan couldn't shake off an uneasy feeling, though. Her intuition wasn't often wrong, and right now, it was signaling that something big was about to happen.

Her gaze returned to the window and the dark woods beyond. The wind whistled through the trees, the leaves rustling like whispered secrets. Her fingers unconsciously moved to the obsidian amulet around her neck to trace the smooth surface.

She mentally reviewed their plan again, preparing for every possible scenario. They had their herbs and crystals ready. Fiona had infused several rocks with energy, turning them into weapons. Jolene was primed to unleash her energy blasts. They'd covered themselves with agrimony, and Fiona had the burlap bag of stones secured to her belt.

They were as prepared as they could be, but Morgan knew that in their world, things rarely went according to plan. The element of surprise was often both their greatest weapon and their biggest threat.

The woods bordering the Blackmoore estate churned with inexplicable oddities. Morgan could only stare as a stag, impressive with its antler crown bearing an uncanny adornment of velvet-soft feathers, emerged from the forest's ebony canvas.

"Darn," she muttered, her pulse thundering in her ears. The buck, wild-eyed and trembling, cast a frantic glance toward the mansion before bolting back into the shadowy wilderness. "What in the world?"

"The magic is getting stronger, spreading farther," Jolene said.

"How much longer should we wait?" Luke asked. "It's getting late and—"

He stopped abruptly when a figure appeared at the edge of the cliff overlooking their property. Maynard

Dove. His movements were cautious, his eyes scanning the area as he walked toward the forest.

"One down, one to go," Cal said.

Only a few more minutes passed before another figure emerged from a different part of their property. The unmistakable flutter of a green cloak gave away Sofie Dove's presence even before they could see her face. Her expression was one of grim determination, a stark contrast to Maynard's wary demeanor.

Jolene's silhouette darkened the window, her gaze trained on the outside world. "Showtime," she declared, her words slicing through the room's stillness. She pivoted, her eyes ablaze with resolve and an undercurrent of exhilaration.

Their plan was about to be tested.

CHAPTER 26

Everyone headed toward the door, senses heightened. Belladonna wound between their legs before slipping out the open door into the night.

They crossed the lawn in tense silence. At the edge of the woods, Morgan halted and peered into the shadowy forest. The trees were hunched and gnarled, branches clawing at the starry sky. Dark spaces yawned between their twisted trunks. The air vibrated with a strange energy.

"Be vigilant," Luke murmured. "I don't like this." His hand rested on Morgan's shoulder.

Morgan steeled herself. "Let's go. But stay close."

They moved into the woods, boots scuffing on leaf litter. Jake unclipped a flashlight from his belt, casting a pale cone of light ahead. Celeste held the celestrolabe up to her eyes with one hand and the lumiscope with the other, fiddling with the gears to tune in the ley lines. The woods pressed close, filled with odd sounds.

"I don't remember the trees being so twisted," Fiona whispered.

Morgan nodded. "The alignment is affecting everything."

They crept deeper, guided by Celeste. "The lines are easier to see. Sofie must be distracted. But the lines feel... agitated."

Indeed, the very air thrummed with nervous energy. Belladonna's eyes glowed as she slipped between shadows.

Jolene gasped. "Look!"

Just ahead, the earth gaped open, a swirling portal rimmed in violet light. They crossed it warily. More portals dotted the woods, gaping like hungry mouths.

"This is worse than before," Mateo muttered.

"But the agrimony is working." Morgan gestured to where Belladonna sat calmly atop a portal. "As long as we have that, we'll be okay."

Nevertheless, they quickened their pace.

"Sofie and Maynard can't be far ahead now," Morgan breathed.

Fiona nodded. "But what will we do when we catch them? We can't force them to cooperate."

"Let's just hope they realize how crucial it is to work together," Luke said. "Neither wants the alignment to cause chaos."

They crept onward, boots crunching softly on twigs. The trees seemed to lean in closer as their branches twisted overhead. Morgan peered into the gloom. She caught a glimpse of emerald green—Sofie's cape—flapping between the trees up ahead.

Her breath caught. "There she is."

Seconds later, a high-pitched scream split the air. "You! You're causing more harm than good!"

"Looks like Sofie ran into Maynard," Jolene said as they all rushed forward.

The group crept closer, the air growing dense with energy. Morgan's hair stood on end, the charged atmosphere sending shivers down her spine.

Up ahead, Maynard and Sofie faced each other, a barrier of crackling energy between them. Their faces were twisted in concentration, eyes blazing with defiance and fury.

"Maynard! Sofie!" Morgan shouted, raising her voice over the sound of hissing energy.

"Stay out of this, Blackmoores!" Maynard barked without turning his head. "This is a family matter."

The ground beneath them vibrated with the force of their power. It felt as though the very earth was shaking in response to their feud. Morgan glanced at her sisters, whose faces reflected her own worry.

Beyond Maynard and Sofie, a large rock sat at the center of the forest. Suspended above it were clusters of yellow crystals spinning furiously like a whirlwind caught in amber light. They pulsed with a blinding radiance that lit up the forest around them. Clearly, this was the epicenter.

Celeste, armed with the celestrolabe and lumiscope, looked horrified as she peered through the ancient instruments. "The ley lines are contorting," she warned, her voice strained with urgency. "They're reacting to Maynard and Sofie's feud. If this keeps up... we may only have minutes before everything erupts!"

Suddenly, Belladonna leapt into the air, batting at the energy patterns with an almost playful determination.

"Belladonna is trying to bat them away from converging!" Celeste said. "But it's too much. We need to do something else."

Morgan tried to reason with Sofie and Maynard, but her pleas fell on deaf ears as the Doves continued their magical standoff. Each attempt to approach was thwarted by an invisible wall of energy that sent the Blackmoores stumbling backward.

"I can intervene," Jolene proposed, her gaze fixed on the intense clash between Maynard and Sofie. "I can use my energy to push the ley lines apart."

Celeste shook her head, the light from the spinning crystals casting eerie shadows on her face. "It's too unpredictable, Jolene. You can't see them like Belladonna and I can. It's too dangerous."

"The energy around them is too volatile! I can't get to the epicenter." Fiona held up the burlap bag containing the stones they hoped would mitigate the power of the alignment.

"It's a shame we can't just make them see how much they care for each other," Jolene said, "Like Mom said she used to do for us."

Jolene's words sparked an idea in Morgan's mind. "Cover me," she instructed, already moving toward the forest's edge.

"Morgan, what are you doing?" Celeste called out in alarm.

"Just trust me," Morgan replied, disappearing into the shadows of the undergrowth.

Her heart pounded as she maneuvered stealthily through the dense foliage. Every crackle of a twig underfoot felt like a gunshot in the tension of the woods.

Sofie was still locked in her power struggle with Maynard when Morgan reappeared behind her. The forest provided ample camouflage as Morgan picked up a hefty log lying nearby.

"Sofie!" Maynard yelled in warning as Morgan hurled the log with all her might.

It happened in slow motion. The log hit Sofie. She crumpled to the ground, her green cloak billowing around her like a leaf caught in a storm. Maynard's shock quickly morphed into fear as he darted toward his fallen sister.

"MORGAN!" Jolene shouted, rushing toward her. "What have you done?"

"Maynard needed to see what he was risking," Morgan explained, her voice shaky. "He needed to understand what he stood to lose."

"But you could have killed her!" Fiona cried, her face pale under the forest's strange glow.

"I didn't throw it that hard," Morgan assured them.

The forest was eerily quiet, the only sound Maynard's ragged breathing as he held his sister close. His eyes met Morgan's across the clearing, and for a moment, there was a flicker of understanding between them.

It had been a desperate move, but it had achieved its purpose. The energy in the air had shifted palpably —it was no longer bristling with tension but trembling with hope.

"Sofie?" Maynard's voice was barely a whisper as his sister's eyes fluttered open. He cradled her in his arms, his face a mask of relief.

"I'm okay," Sofie murmured, reaching up to touch his cheek. "You... you were worried about me."

Maynard's lips twitched in a semblance of a smile. "You're my sister. What did you expect?"

Sofie blinked up at him, her eyes filling with tears. "I thought you'd seize the opportunity to take control of the lines."

"Well, I guess we both learned something today," Maynard said softly.

A shadow fell over them, and they looked up to see Jolene standing there, her arms crossed over her chest. "This is a real touching family reunion," she said, "but we have a problem."

She pointed toward the spinning stones over the epicenter. The stones were still rotating wildly, casting eerie shadows on the surrounding trees.

Morgan stepped forward, her eyes flicking

between Sofie and Maynard. "Are you two ready to put your differences aside and help us control this?"

Maynard and Sofie exchanged a glance before nodding in unison.

"Good," Morgan said. She turned to the others. "Let's get to work."

They moved with newfound determination, working together to clear a path through the ley lines toward the epicenter. Fiona was at the front, using her magical abilities to guide them safely through.

When they reached the epicenter, Fiona pulled the stones from the burlap bag and placed them precisely, each one radiating a soothing energy that seemed to calm the frenzied ley lines and dim the glow of the yellow crystals.

The change was immediate and palpable. The air lightened around them, the oppressive weight of tension lifting as if a switch had been flipped. Birds began to chirp in the trees overhead, their melodies bright and cheerful.

"Did it work?" Morgan asked tentatively. After the chaos of the last few hours, she hardly dared believe they had succeeded.

Celeste nodded, lowering the celestrolabe. "The ley lines have calmed significantly. Placing the stones disrupted their pattern enough to dampen the effects of the alignment."

"For now, at least," Luke added. He put a steadying hand on Morgan's shoulder. "We'll have to wait and see if it holds through midnight, when the alignment peaks."

"So what do we do until then?" Jolene asked.

"We should head back to the house and keep an eye on things," she suggested. "Make sure nothing changes between now and midnight."

The others murmured agreement.

"I'll come with you," Maynard said gruffly. He was supporting Sofie with one arm. "Just until we're sure there's no more trouble coming."

Sofie gave a tired smile. "I think we've caused enough trouble for one day."

Jolene rolled her eyes but didn't argue as they began making their way out of the forest. The journey back was far less fraught than their trip in had been. With the ley lines stabilized, the portals had disappeared, and the trees no longer clawed at them as they passed.

As they emerged from the forest, Calvin turned to Sofie and Maynard, who were walking side by side. "So what was your feud about anyway?"

Sofie and Maynard stopped and looked at each

other. Their brows furrowed in thought, and then they both shrugged.

"You know," Sofie said, "I can't quite remember."

Maynard chuckled. "Neither can I."

Morgan smiled at their exchange, feeling a sense of relief wash over her. They had done it. They had worked together to prevent a disaster, and in doing so, they had helped mend a centuries-old feud between Maynard and Sofie. For the first time in a long while, things were looking up.

Morgan relaxed in her wicker chair, gazing at the flickering flames in the firepit. She savored the smoky aroma of the crackling fire. Across from Morgan sat her sisters Celeste, Jolene, and Fiona on similar chairs, their faces illuminated in the firelight.

Luke put his arm around Morgan, and she leaned against him. "It's almost time," he said softly. Morgan nodded, feeling both eager and apprehensive for the midnight hour.

Celeste sighed. "I hope we're doing the right thing. What if what we did makes it worse?"

"It'll work," Jolene said confidently. "We planned this perfectly."

Calvin stepped out from the house, holding a tray of mugs. "Hot cider, anyone?"

"Ooh, yes, please!" Fiona said, taking a mug. The others followed suit, sipping the warm cider under the clear night sky.

Jake stretched and yawned. "Well, if I pass out, someone wake me at midnight."

"Don't worry. I'll keep you awake," Fiona teased.

Jake grinned. "I knew I could count on you."

Sofie patted Maynard's hand. "We cannot thank you all enough for bringing us together again."

Morgan met Sofie's grateful gaze. "We're just happy that things got resolved."

Maynard chuckled. "All it took was a few centuries of feuding, stolen artifacts, and an impending apocalypse."

"And a little bump on my head." Sofie patted the back of her head and laughed.

Celeste glanced at her watch. "Eleven fifty-eight. Just two minutes to go!"

The group tensed, turning their focus to the forest, which was barely visible in the moonlight. They waited.

"Here we go," Mateo murmured. He and Jolene joined hands.

Johanna sipped her cider. "Everything will be fine."

At that moment, the clocks struck midnight. A pulse of energy rippled out from the woods like a shock wave. A flock of white doves burst out of the forest and flew off into the night. The wind gusted, blowing hair and rustling leaves. Morgan's amulet grew warm against her chest.

Then, just as suddenly, the wind died down. The night stilled. Crickets tentatively resumed their chorus.

Fiona looked around. "Did it...work?"

Morgan stood slowly, gazing toward the trees. "I think...yes. The magical energy feels stabilized, harmonious."

Celeste beamed, barely able to contain her excitement. "We did it!"

"Woo-hoo!" Fiona cheered, giving Jake a high five.

Jolene pumped her fist. "I knew we could do it!"

"Well done," Maynard said warmly.

"This calls for a celebration!" Calvin declared, heading inside to grab a bottle of champagne.

Before Calvin got halfway to the house, the sound of sirens pierced the peaceful night air. Red and blue lights flashed through the trees as a police cruiser came screeching up the long driveway in front of the house.

Sheriff White appeared around the corner, hand

on her hip near her holster. "We got a call about some kinda disturbance out here. Wanna tell me what's going on?"

Morgan exchanged a nervous glance with her sisters before replying. "Oh, nothing, Sheriff. We were just having a little celebration with some friends."

Sheriff White raised an eyebrow. "Is that right? Neighbors said they heard fireworks."

"Fireworks?" Fiona said innocently. "No, we were just having some cider by the fire."

"Really?" White seemed skeptical as she glanced around the lawn. "Fireworks require a permit, and you don't have one."

"That's because we weren't lighting them off," Jolene said in an exasperated tone.

White scanned the group, her narrow-eyed gaze settling on Sofie and Maynard. "Well, isn't this interesting. Finding you two here after you accused Mr. Reed and the Blackmoores of stealing your property."

Maynard smiled politely. "It was all just a misunderstanding. I spoke with Calvin here, and we cleared everything up."

Sheriff White looked unconvinced. "Uh-huh. Well, you folks best keep it down, whatever it is you're up to out here." She gave the group a pointed look. "Don't think I won't be keeping an eye on you. I know you're up to something."

The group let out a collective sigh of relief as the flashing lights disappeared into the night.

"Well, now, I guess we can all really use this." Calvin held up the two bottles of champagne.

They popped the cork and filled paper cups. Belladonna wound between everyone's legs, purring loudly.

"To new friends and allies." Sofie raised her glass, nodding to Maynard.

"To second chances," Maynard added.

More cheers went up as they sipped champagne. The crisp night air rang with laughter and lively conversation recounting the night's events.

As things wound down, Luke checked his phone and grinned. "Message from Dorian—'Excellent work. The agency is impressed.'"

Jake whistled. "Look at us, impressing secret government agencies."

Morgan sighed contentedly, snuggling against Luke. Out of the corner of her eye, she noticed a tiny snail inching across a leaf, its minuscule feet extended comically.

Wait... feet? She leaned forward for a better look and practically fell out of her chair.

"Whoa, there." Luke pulled her back. "What's wrong?"

"Wrong?" Morgan looked at him innocently. "Oh, nothing." She glanced back at the snail. Yep, it definitely had feet. Probably just some overflow magic from before the alignment. Nothing to worry about. "Nothing at all."

****

If you liked the Blackmoore Sisters, you might enjoy my Silver Hollow series. Check out Book 1, A Spell of Trouble here.

Connect on Facebook - Join my private readers group on Facebook and get a sneak peek at what I'm working on plus connect with like-minded readers and discuss our favorite books:

https://www.facebook.com/groups/ldobbsreaders

SEE all Leighann Dobbs series here -> http://www.leighanndobbsbooks.com

ALSO BY LEIGHANN DOBBS

Cozy Mysteries

Moorecliff Manor Cat Cozy Mystery Series

* * *

Dead in the Dining Room

Stabbed in the Solarium

Homicide in the Hydrangeas

Lifeless in the Library

Mayhem in the Mudroom

Mystic Notch

Cat Cozy Mystery Series

* * *

* * *

Ghostly Paws

A Spirited Tail

A Mew To A Kill

Paws and Effect

Probable Paws

A Whisker of a Doubt

Wrong Side of the Claw

Claw and Order

Juniper Holiday Cozy Mysteries

***

Halloween Party Murder

Thanksgiving Dinner Death

Who Slayed The Santas?

Masquerade Party Murder

My Fatal Valentine

Oyster Cove Guesthouse

Cat Cozy Mystery Series

***

A Twist in the Tail

A Whisker in the Dark

A Purrfect Alibi

Kate Diamond Mystery Adventures

***

Hidden Agemda (Book 1)

Ancient Hiss Story (Book 2)

Heist Society (Book 3)

Silver Hollow

Paranormal Cozy Mystery Series

***

A Spell of Trouble (Book 1)

Spell Disaster (Book 2)

Nothing to Croak About (Book 3)

Cry Wolf (Book 4)

Shear Magic (Book 5)

Mooseamuck Island

Cozy Mystery Series

* * *

A Zen For Murder

A Crabby Killer

A Treacherous Treasure

Blackmoore Sisters

Cozy Mystery Series

* * *

Dead Wrong

Dead & Buried

Dead Tide

Buried Secrets

Deadly Intentions

A Grave Mistake

Spell Found

Fatal Fortune

Hidden Secrets

Celestial Chaos

Lexy Baker

Cozy Mystery Series

* * *

Killer Cupcakes

Dying For Danish

Murder, Money and Marzipan

3 Bodies and a Biscotti

Brownies, Bodies & Bad Guys

Bake, Battle & Roll

Wedded Blintz

Scones, Skulls & Scams

Ice Cream Murder

Mummified Meringues

Brutal Brulee (Novella)

No Scone Unturned

Cream Puff Killer

Never Say Pie

Ain't Seen Muffin Yet

Assault and Buttercream

Lady Katherine Regency Mysteries

***

An Invitation to Murder (Book 1)

The Baffling Burglaries of Bath (Book 2)

Murder at the Ice Ball (Book 3)

A Murderous Affair (Book 4)

Murder on Charles Street (Book 5)

Julia and Nora Marsh 1920s Cozy Mystery

***

Murder on a Mississippi Steamboat

Hazel Martin Historical Mystery Series

***

Murder at Lowry House (book 1)

Murder by Misunderstanding (book 2)

Sam Mason Mysteries

(As L. A. Dobbs)

***

Telling Lies (Book 1)

Keeping Secrets (Book 2)

Exposing Truths (Book 3)

Betraying Trust (Book 4)

Killing Dreams (Book 5)

More books in the Rockford Security Series:

Cold As Her Heart

A Game of Kill

No One To Trust

No Time To Run

Don't Fear The Truth

Hide From The Past

Romantic Comedy

***

Corporate Chaos Series

In Over Her Head (book 1)

Can't Stand the Heat (book 2)

What Goes Around Comes Around (book 3)

Careful What You Wish For (4)

Dish Best Served Cold (5)

Contemporary Romance

***

Reluctant Romance

Sweet Romance (Written As Annie Dobbs)

Firefly Inn Series

***

Another Chance (Book 1)

Another Wish (Book 2)

Hometown Hearts Series

***

No Getting Over You (Book 1)

A Change of Heart (Book 2)

Sweet Mountain Billionaires

***

Jaded Billionaire (Book 1)

A Billion Reasons Not To Fall In Love (Book 2)

***

Sweetrock Sweet and Spicy Cowboy Romance

Some Like It Hot

Too Close For Comfort

———

Regency Romance

* * *

Scandals and Spies Series:

Kissing The Enemy

Deceiving the Duke

Tempting the Rival

Charming the Spy

Pursuing the Traitor

Captivating the Captain

The Unexpected Series:

An Unexpected Proposal

An Unexpected Passion

Dobbs Fancytales:

Dobbs Fancytales Boxed Set Collection

————

Western Historical Romance

***

Goldwater Creek Mail Order Brides:

Faith

American Mail Order Brides Series:

Chevonne: Bride of Oklahoma

————————————

Magical Romance with a Touch of Mystery

***

Something Magical

Curiously Enchanted

ABOUT THE AUTHOR

USA Today Bestselling author Leighann Dobbs has had a passion for reading since she was old enough to hold a book, but she didn't put pen to paper until much later in life. After a twenty-year career as a software engineer with a few side trips into selling antiques and making jewelry, she realized you can't make a living reading books, so she tried her hand at writing them and discovered she had a passion for that, too! She lives in New Hampshire with her husband, Bruce, their trusty Chihuahua mix, Mojo, and beautiful rescue cat, Kitty.

Her book "Dead Wrong" won the "Best Mystery Romance" award at the 2014 Indie Romance Convention.

Her book "Ghostly Paws" was the 2015 Chanticleer Mystery & Mayhem First Place category winner in the Animal Mystery category.

Join her VIP Readers group on Facebook:

https://www.facebook.com/groups/ldobbsreaders

This is a work of fiction.

None of it is real. All names, places, and events are products of the author's imagination. Any resemblance to real names, places, or events are purely coincidental, and should not be construed as being real.

Celestial Chaos

Copyright © 2024

Leighann Dobbs Publishing

All Rights Reserved.

No part of this work may be used or reproduced in any manner, except as allowable under "fair use," without the express written permission of the author.

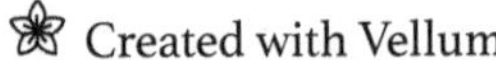 Created with Vellum